GRIM DEA

Rich Mrs. Mallaby is hated by almost everyone in the village of Long Manton. When she is murdered in the church, Superintendent Hockley is faced with a big problem — nearly everybody has a motive. And what about the five hundred pounds which the dead woman had drawn out of her account? It looks like blackmail — but is it? Best-selling author Peter Hunt lives in the village, and is determined to solve the problem . . .

GERALD VERNER

GRIM DEATH

Complete and Unabridged

LINFORD
Leicester

First published in Great Britain

First Linford Edition
published 2013

A catalogue record for this book is available
from the British Library.

ISBN 978–1–4448–1726–3

Published by
F. A. Thorpe (Publishing)
Anstey, Leicestershire

Set by Words & Graphics Ltd.
Anstey, Leicestershire
Printed and bound in Great Britain by
T. J. International Ltd., Padstow, Cornwall

This book is printed on acid-free paper

1

Peter Hunt stopped in the welcome shade of a tree and lit a cigarette. It was very hot, and he wished that he had not been persuaded by his sister to attend the vicarage garden party that afternoon.

The clock in the tower of St. Mary's Church reminded him that he must make a move if he did not want to be late, and regretfully leaving the shade of the accommodating tree he set off down the scorching road.

When he got to the vicarage gate he could hear the sounds of chattering voices from beyond and felt even less anxious to join the owners than he had before. However, it had to be done, and opening the gate he walked up the smooth gravel path and under an arch in the clipped yew hedge. Beyond, under a wide-spreading cedar, groups of people were sitting or standing about on the smooth-shaven lawn, sipping tea and eating sandwiches and cakes served by a small servant from an extempore buffet presided over by the vicar's wife.

Peter looked about for his sister and presently saw her sitting between the bank manager and Miss Dewsnap, the village postmistress. He was going over to join her when he was accosted by the vicar, a large and benign man of imposing stature.

'Delighted to see you,' purred the Reverend Mr. Popkiss with great unction. He always reminded Peter of a lump of margarine that had got soft in the sun. 'Delighted. How is the new — er — work progressing?'

Nothing annoyed Peter more than having his novels referred to as 'works'. He was a professional writer who wrote for a living and had no illusions that his books were any more than entertaining to the general public. He murmured that it was coming along well.

'Splendid, splendid,' said the Reverend Mr. Popkiss, and to Peter's relief he passed on to speak to another of his parishioners. Peter avoided Olive Popkiss, the vicar's rather lumpy daughter, and succeeded in reaching his sister without further molestation.

'You look hot,' she remarked as he dragged up a vacant deck-chair and sat down beside her, Mr. Withers, the bank manager, a little nervous man, making room for him.

'I *am* hot,' said Peter. 'How do you do, Miss Dewsnap? How do you do, Withers?'

The angular Miss Dewsnap remarked that the heat was rather trying, and Mr. Withers said that he was quite well.

He didn't look it. He looked rather harassed, as he always did. Peter always felt sorry for Horace Withers. His strength and personality had been sucked completely away by the woman he had married. Mrs. Withers and her daughter, Diana, were selfish and demanding. They expected everything from the man who worked like a lumberjack to provide for their needs and seldom got a thank you for his pains.

'If you want any tea,' said Margaret, stretching out her legs, 'you'd better grab

Agnes before it's all gone.'

Peter looked round at the small maid staggering under a large tray filled with sandwiches and cups of tea who was passing just behind him. He got up, helped himself to a sandwich and a cup of rather weak tea, and sat down again. They all four chatted rather desultorily for a few minutes and then Mr. Withers and Miss Dewsnap went over to talk to some other people and they were left to themselves.

'The usual menagerie,' said Peter unkindly, looking about him. 'All the old exhibits.'

'Including Mrs. Mallaby,' said Margaret. She nodded to where a stout and majestic figure was enthroned in a deck-chair and surrounded by a group of admiring sycophants.

'She's the worst of the lot,' declared Peter with a grimace. 'I detest that woman. She's a mental sadist.'

Mrs. Mallaby, as though she knew that he was talking about her, turned her small eyes towards him and graciously inclined her head. It was like a royal greeting, a queen acknowledging a humble subject.

Peter bowed in return, grunting something under his breath that his sister failed to catch.

A tall, thinnish man, very dapper, with rather faded and prominent blue eyes and a carefully brushed moustache, came up to them.

'Good afternoon, Colonel Bramber,' said Margaret with a charming but completely insincere smile, 'I suppose you feel quite at home in this heat?'

'Wouldn't go so far as that,' answered Colonel Bramber in a slightly hoarse voice. 'Different kind of heat in India, y'know. Dry. None of this humidity.'

'I feel absolutely limp,' said Margaret. 'How is your wife? Is she better?'

The Colonel shook his head.

''Fraid not,' he said. 'Didn't feel equal to comin' out in this heat. Asked me to come, though. Not much in my line this sort of thin'.' He waved a hand vaguely about him.

'I don't expect there's anything the matter with her at all,' thought Peter. 'Just too lazy to get off the settee.' He knew Mrs. Bramber. She was always suffering from some unidentified complaint which prevented her from doing anything that she didn't want to. It was very convenient.

'Do remember me to her, won't you?' said Margaret sweetly but with a hint of dismissal in her voice.

'And me,' said Peter.

'Most kind of you both,' said the Colonel. 'Why not drop in one evenin', eh? Have a rubber or so of bridge . . . '

'I'm terribly busy just now,' broke in Peter hastily. 'In the middle of a new book, you know.'

'I know, I know,' said Colonel Bramber with a look of disappointment. 'Oh well, when you feel like a spot of relaxation . . . No need to stand on ceremony, you know. Just drop in an' take pot luck . . . any time.'

'That's awfully kind of you, Colonel Bramber,' said Margaret.

Colonel Bramber hesitated for a moment, bowed, and drifted rather wistfully away.

'He's not so bad, even if his bridge is,' said Peter, looking after him. 'It's the female of the species. She can talk about nothing else but India and how many servants they had and her infernal ailments. How long do we have to stay?'

'We can't go *just* yet,' said his sister. 'Do look at Olive Popkiss,' she added as the vicar's daughter crossed the lawn to her mother at the buffet. 'She really is the ugliest girl I think I've ever seen. She walks just like a duck.'

'You're catching the general complaint of cattiness,' said her brother. 'That's the sort of thing Mrs. Mallaby would say.'

The hot afternoon wore slowly on and at last people began to leave. Peter and Margaret, with great relief and a sense of having done their duty, said goodbye to the vicar, receiving a flabby and rather moist handshake, and set off home.

The annual tea-party was over for another year.

★　★　★

'I think I'll have the window shut, dear,' said Mrs. Bramber plaintively. 'I feel a little chilly.'

It was unpleasantly hot in the low-ceilinged room, but her husband shut the casement windows without argument. Thirty-five years of Mrs. Bramber had convinced him that argument was futile.

She was a small, faded woman with something remaining of her former prettiness but not much. She lay on a cushioned divan beside a low table laden with books and magazines and a large box of Turkish delight of which she consumed large quantities in the intervals of discussing her health.

'I don't think I shall ever feel really well in this country,' she continued, popping a large piece of Turkish delight into her discontented mouth. 'It's the climate, I suppose. I always felt well in India.'

Her husband might have replied that with a number of native servants to carry out her every wish there was no need for her to have felt anything else, but he contented himself with a grunt.

'Saw the Hunts this afternoon,' he said. 'Asked 'em to drop in for a rubber of bridge . . . '

'Oh, not this evening, dear,' broke in

his wife. 'I do think you're a little inconsiderate. How can you expect me to entertain people in my state of health . . . ?'

'Needn't get worried. They're not coming,' grunted the Colonel. 'Hunt's busy on a new book or somethin'. Thought it might cheer you up a bit . . .'

'I couldn't bear anyone, dear,' declared Mrs. Bramber. 'You know the only thing that does me any good when I have one of my attacks is complete rest and quiet . . .'

'Well, it's all right. I've told you they're not coming,' said her husband.

'I know it must be very dull for you dear,' said Mrs. Bamber plaintively, 'but I really cannot help it. It's no pleasure to me to always feel so weak and limp . . .'

'No, no, shocking for you. Must be beastly,' said the Colonel hastily. He had made the mistake once, but only once, of suggesting that perhaps she would feel better if she were a trifle more energetic. For a week after she had been so ill that she had been confined to her bed and he had had to wait on her practically hand and foot.

'What was the party like?' she asked.

'The usual sort of thing,' said the Colonel. 'Glad when it was over.'

'That dreadful woman, Mrs. Mallaby was there, I suppose?' said Mrs. Bramber, frowning. 'A most unpleasant woman. Why she should set herself up as a paragon, I *don't* know. Do you remember how insulting she was to me when I was telling her about Pondicherry?'

'Yes, yes, my dear,' broke in the Colonel soothingly. 'Most uncalled for . . .'

'She's an odious creature,' declared Mrs. Bramber, sustaining her strength with another piece of Turkish delight. 'Everybody in Long Manton hates her . . . I think I should like the window open again, dear. It seems to have got quite close all of a sudden.'

Dutifully, Colonel Bramber complied with her request.

* * *

'Some more salad?' asked Mrs. Conway.

Her husband looked at the big glass

bowl thoughtfully and nodded.

'I will,' he answered. 'You make a very fine salad, Mary, a very fine salad indeed.'

His wife laughed.

'You always say that,' she said, pouring out a fresh cup of tea.

'And each time it's more true than the last,' he declared. 'When it comes to things like that and cooking there's not many can beat you.'

'The way to a man's heart is through his stomach, they say,' she replied. She reached for his cup and poured him out some more tea. For a little while there was silence in the pleasant, comfortable room. Mr. Conway finished his second helping of salad, drank his tea, and lit a cigarette with complete contentment.

'That was a better cup of tea than the wishy-washy stuff they gave us this afternoon,' he remarked, blowing out a cloud of smoke.

'And drunk in better surroundings,' said his wife. 'I can't stand all those old tabbies who flock round the vicar. Especially Mrs. Mallaby.'

'You could scarcely call her an old

tabby,' said Conway. 'She's a very forceful and formidable woman.'

'She's horrible,' said Mrs. Conway. 'She takes a delight in hurting people. A lot of the people round here crawl to her because she's got money and lives in the big house, but I'm sure they all hate her really. Her tongue is always being spiteful about someone.'

'I just don't bother about her,' said Mr. Conway, shrugging his shoulders.

'You would, if she started talking about us the same as she does about other people,' said his wife.

'I expect she has,' replied her husband, 'but there isn't much she can say, is there?'

'There might be quite a lot, if she only knew,' said Mrs. Conway quietly, and her husband's face changed.

'I don't see how she could know about that,' he answered gravely. 'Nobody knows about that — except ourselves. It rather worries me sometimes . . . '

'It doesn't worry me,' said Mrs. Conway quickly. She got up and began to collect the dirty supper things. 'Let's forget Mrs. Mallaby and all the rest of them. We're quite happy without them.'

Mr. Conway got up too. He put his arm round her waist and kissed her.

'Sure you're quite happy, Mary?' he asked, looking searchingly into her upturned face.

'Quite sure,' she answered. 'Quite, quite sure.'

'I'll help you wash up,' said her husband.

★   ★   ★

The Reverend Mr. Popkiss held up a glass of port to the light, twisting it delicately in his fingers.

'Well,' he said in a tone of satisfaction, '*that's* over for another year.'

'Yes, indeed,' declared his wife. 'I am feeling quite exhausted. It seems to get more exhausting each year.'

'We do our duty,' remarked the Reverend Mr. Popkiss with satisfaction. 'We do our duty, my dear.'

'And everybody is very glad when it's all over,' interposed Olive. 'They all hate it, really, you know. Except that awful woman, Mrs. Mallaby.'

'You must not speak like that, Olive,' said the vicar. 'Mrs. Mallaby is a most devout churchwoman.'

'She's a nasty old cat!' said Olive. 'Always spying and telling tales about people . . . '

'Hold your tongue, Olive,' said her mother. 'I won't have you talking like that.'

'Everybody knows it's true, all the same,' said Olive sullenly. 'She's a horrible, vindictive, malicious old beast.'

'Olive, that will do,' said her father sharply. 'What has come over you? You've never been like this before.'

Her eyes filled with tears. She got up from the table abruptly and almost ran out of the room.

The Reverend Mr. Popkiss stared after her in astonishment.

* * *

Mrs. Withers lay back in a deep armchair and wiggled her toes in an ecstasy of relief. Her shoes, which had been hurting her all that hot afternoon, lay on the rug where she had kicked them off.

'Why don't you wear shoes that fit you, Mother?' asked her daughter, Diana, languidly from the depths of the settee on which she lay at full length.

'These would fit me normally,' answered Mrs. Withers, 'but my feet always swell with the heat. You know that.'

'If it isn't heat, it's chilblains,' retorted Diana unkindly. She reached for a cigarette from the table near her and stuck it between her scarlet lips. Her lighter was in her handbag which she had put down on a table by the window.

'Daddy,' she called. 'Daddy!'

'Yes, my dear?' The voice of Mr. Withers floated through the open door from the direction of the kitchen.

'Bring me a light,' called Diana.

There was a short pause and Mr. Withers came in. He had removed his jacket and rolled up his shirt-sleeves, and he was wearing an apron which he had tied round his middle. His sparse hair was disordered. He struck a match and held it to his daughter's cigarette.

'Thanks,' she said briefly.

'How long will dinner be?' asked Mrs. Withers.

'About twenty minutes, my dear,' said Mr. Withers with his usual slight stammer. 'The potatoes are on and I've made the s-salad. I'm just going to lay the table.'

'You might give me a gin and orange,' said Diana. 'I'm gasping.'

'And me,' put in Mrs. Withers. 'I need something to take away the taste of the vicarage tea.'

'Ghastly, wasn't it?' said Diana. 'I always hate that sort of do.'

'It gets worse every year,' said her mother. 'I'm sure Mrs. Popkiss keeps an inferior-quality tea for the occasion.'

Mr. Withers brought over two glasses. He gave one to his wife and one to his daughter. They took them with hardly a word of thanks and he quietly slipped back to the kitchen.

'Mrs. Mallaby was in full fettle,' said Diana. 'Like old Queen Elizabeth holding court.'

'I really detest that woman,' declared Mrs. Withers. When they had first come to Long Manton, after Mr. Withers had been appointed manager of the bank, Mrs. Withers had done her very best to become an intimate friend of Mrs. Mallaby's, for that lady had by far the largest account of anybody in the village. But Mrs. Mallaby had met all her gushing advances with an icy coolness that made it quite plain that she had no wish to become friendly with the bank manager's wife. Since then Mrs. Withers never had a good word to say about her.

She and her daughter discussed the various people of the village while Mr. Withers watched anxiously over the potatoes for dinner. He was a greatly worried little man. The luxuries demanded by his wife and daughter left no margin available from his modest income for a maid's wages and, since neither Mrs. Withers nor Diana would demean themselves by doing a hand's turn if they could help it, the work of the small house devolved almost entirely to him.

He got up every morning at half-past six and did what cleaning was necessary before getting tea and breakfast — in the winter he lit the fires — and leaving the vegetables ready for lunch. He took two trays up to his wife and daughter so that they could have their breakfast in the ease and comfort of their respective beds. When he came home in the evening, after his day's work, he prepared the dinner, cleared it away and washed up. After that he was free to work on such of the local accounts as had been entrusted to him and which brought him in a little extra money. Sometimes it was one or two in the morning before he crept up the stairs to his own small bedroom with weary eyes and an aching head. Nobody would have cared if he stopped up all night. He was nothing in the house except a machine that brought in money — tolerated without being considered. It never crossed his mind that he was badly treated. He accepted things as they were and was immensely proud of his good-looking wife and flamboyant daughter, his only ambition in life being to gratify their extravagant demands. As time went on this became increasingly difficult. His expenditure insisted on leaping ahead of his income so that in order to balance his budget he had to practise rigid economy, cutting out at length even his tobacco, which was his only luxury, and taking on more and more outside work.

Patient, hard-working, uncomplaining, Mr. Withers shouldered the responsibilities which were so heavy that his narrow shoulders could scarcely carry the burden, deserving something better than he got in return for his unselfish devotion.

★　★　★

Mrs. Mallaby sat at the small desk in her drawing-room and went methodically through the monthly accounts. The late Mr. Mallaby had died leaving the whole of his huge fortune, which he had acquired by the manufacture of a purgative pill, to his wife.

In spite of the fact that her annual income was more than the Prime Minister's salary, Mrs. Mallaby was very mean. She personally weighed every particle of food that came into Manton Lodge, and woe betide the unfortunate tradesman who gave short measure. She found it very difficult to keep servants, for she was a hard mistress who never gave praise but only blame. She had a habit, too, of going from room to room looking for dust. If she found any a shilling would be docked from the servant's wages who had been responsible for this slovenliness.

In consequence, the servants hated her. They feared her too, for her tongue could hurt like a whip-lash.

Mrs. Mallaby, however, was impervious to hatred or dislike from anybody. She was a law unto herself and cared not one iota what people said or thought about her. She had a habit of putting the worst construction on anyone's motives and her rigid outlook brooked of no half measures. A thing was either right or it was wrong — there were no extenuating circumstances with Mrs. Mallaby. And she took a delight in seeing people suffer. She would not have admitted this, but it was true.

Not a nice woman, universally disliked and hated by all who knew her, but satisfied with herself and her mode of life to the point of complacency. Well fed, tranquil and contented, no faint shadow came to warn her that her days in the land were numbered and that she had very little longer to live.

2

Peter Hunt came slowly down the hill to the village in the dusk of the summer evening. He walked unhurriedly, enjoying the quiet beauty that surrounded him.

It was cool and peaceful after the heat of the day. Another day of heat even hotter than the day of the vicarage tea-party. A great moon hung low over the trees and the sky was an ever-deepening shade of blue. The scents of the June night drenched the warm, still air, a perfume blent of flowers and hot grass and the tang of baked earth; a magic essence that has in it all the wonder of the earth.

Peter loved the country in all its moods. In mid-winter when the trees were bare of leaf and formed delicate traceries of black against a grey sky, and the air was sharp and cold and clear; when the snow lay thick upon the ground and everything was like an etching in black and white, and when the hoar frost turned hedge and tree and shrub into glittering stands of diamonds; when spring threw a gauzy veil over the austerity of winter, softening every harsh outline and slowly tinting the black and grey and white until they became the flaming colours of summer; when the gradual decay of autumn faded out the deep colours through a last rich blend of russet, yellow, and red, to black and grey once more.

He had planned to go on with his novel that evening but a vague restlessness made work impossible, and he decided to seek the company provided by the Fox and Hounds and solace his restlessness with beer.

The lights in the old inn shone invitingly as he crossed the moonlit Green and he could hear laughter and the friendly sounds of many voices. It was a comforting, soothing sound, and he pushed open the door and entered the low-ceilinged, raftered bar.

A group of villagers were playing a noisy game of darts, and a dozen or so others were standing laughing and talking among themselves and exchanging jokes with the red-faced landlord.

Mr. Penny gave Peter a welcoming grin as he pushed his way to the bar.

'Good evening, sir,' he greeted. 'A pint of the usual, is it?'

'It is,' said Peter. 'How are you, Penny?'

'I've felt better an' I've felt worse,' said the landlord as he drew a pint of foaming ale into a tankard and set it down on the bar. 'It's this 'eat that gets me. I wasn't built for 'eat an' it's been powerful 'ot terday — wors'n what it was yesterday.'

'It won't last,' put in a weasel-faced little man, shaking his head. 'We'll get a storm an' then it'll go all of a sudden-like.'

'You've bin sayin' that for the last two weeks,' said the landlord, wiping his shining face with a huge coloured silk handkerchief. 'Nuthin' ain't 'appened yet.'

'It will, you mark my words,' retorted the weasel-faced man.

'Course it will if you go on sayin' it long enough, Snellit,' said one of the others round the bar and there was a general laugh.

'Weather won't break till the change o' the moon,' said a thin man in a cloth cap. 'Ain't that right, Mr. Disher?'

Thus appealed to, Mr. Disher removed the greater part of his face from a tankard of beer and surveyed his questioner with a watery eye.

'Won't break then, if yer asks me,' he said in a husky voice. 'In fer a long spell of it, we are.'

'We could do with a good drop o' rain,' remarked a stout man who looked like, and actually was, a farmer. 'Everythin' in the fields is burnin' up.'

There followed a long discussion on the ruin the weather was doing to the crops and Peter listened in delight, for this was what he enjoyed, this simple life of the countryside. He finished his beer and called for another pint and was served by a chuckling landlord.

'One thing about this weather, it's good fer trade,' said Mr. Penny.

'Your trade, but not mine,' said Mr. Boggs, the butcher, from the back of the little group at the bar. 'Meat's a rare problem to 'andle these 'ot days!'

'First time you'll be sellin' meat that ain't froze solid, Boggs,' called someone and there was a general laugh.

'You will 'ave yer little joke, Mercher,' said Mr. Boggs good-humouredly. 'Everyone knows only the best comes to my shop.'

'Mrs. Mallaby don't think so, Boggs,' remarked Mr. Disher, and the butcher's red face grew even redder.

'She's a woman what's impossible to please,' he said, shaking his head. 'Never satisfied with nuthin'. An' she couldn't get better meat anywhere, though I say it meself.'

'Aye, she's a tartar, she is,' said the farmer. 'Look at all the accidents there've been at the curve in the road where them trees grow so that you can't see what's comin'. Ought to be cut down, they did, but she won't hear of it though she 'ad a deputation from the village. 'They're on my land,' she said, 'and they'll stop where they are'.'

'Best take 'er an' 'ang 'er from one of

'em,' said Mr. Disher. 'That 'ud please us all.'

On this note, Peter took his leave. He had enjoyed the brief break and felt that he could now probably get in an hour or two working on his novel before going to bed.

Margaret was curled up on the big settee in the living-room reading a book when he got back, and she looked up with a smile.

'Hello,' she said, 'had a good time?'

'I feel much better,' he declared, lighting a cigarette.

'Harriet came in just after you went,' said his sister. 'She'd been to see Anthony. The doctor says the danger is past.'

'Oh good,' said Peter. 'When's he likely to be coming home?'

'Some time next week,' answered Margaret.

'It will be nice to see old Anthony again,' said Peter. 'Poor chap, he's had a bad time.'

Anthony and Harriet Medcott were their nearest neighbours, and in the spring of that year Anthony had suffered a serious accident. He had slipped on the polished floor of the dining-room and his head had gone through one of the panes of the French windows. A splinter of glass had been driven into his skull and touched a portion of the brain. It had been a period of grave anxiety for his wife, Harriet, for the specialist she had called in had been very candid about the case. The removal of the splinter would necessitate a delicate and dangerous operation. If the operation was not performed Anthony was likely to remain paralysed for the rest of his life. On the other hand there was only a fifty-fifty chance of it proving successful. Harriet decided that the fifty-fifty chance was worth taking. The operation had been successful, though there had been weeks of anxiety while Anthony hovered on the borderline. Now he was on the way to complete recovery.

'Harriet says he'll have to take it very easily for a month or so,' said Margaret. 'She's going to bring him over for dinner one evening.'

'That'll be fine,' said Peter enthusiastically.

'Harriet's been wonderful, I think,' said Margaret, uncurling her long legs and getting up. 'It must have been a terrible time for her. I'm going to make some coffee and then I'm going to bed. What are you doing? Are you working?'

Peter nodded.

'Yes, for a couple of hours,' he said.

'I'll bring the coffee into the study,' said his sister, and went through to the kitchen.

Peter crossed the wide hall to his study, sat down at his desk, and lit another cigarette. He felt much better for his visit to the Fox and Hounds but there was still, lurking somewhere in the depths of his mind, a vague uneasiness. He couldn't trace it to any particular cause and after a moment he thrust it resolutely away, put a sheet of paper in the typewriter, and settled down to work.

★　★　★

Over the sleeping village that lifeless light which is but the reflected glory of the sun poured down from a nearly full moon,

29

flooding field and street and lane with a brightness that was like the ghost of noon.

It filtered in through a chink in the curtains of Miss Dewsnap's bedroom and indelicately focused on a glass of water in which Miss Dewsnap's teeth had retired for the night. Miss Dewsnap herself lay in her old-fashioned bed, sleeping soundly, and softly vibrating the atmosphere with a genteel snore. It flooded brilliantly through the open window of the room where Mr. and Mrs. Conway slept, for they had forgotten to close the curtains. He was muttering uneasily in his sleep and she had thrown a protecting arm around him as though to ward off any dangers that the night might bring. It shone through the window of the attic room at the vicarage where the little servant, Gladys, slept like a log, tired out by her day's hard work, and came reluctantly and hesitantly, as though diffident of intruding into the presence of such a great man, into the bedchamber of the Reverend Mr. Popkiss. He lay on his back, like the effigy on a crusader's tomb, and breathed heavily and noisily. In the twin bed beside him, Mrs. Popkiss, curled up like the letter Z, emitted a series of peculiar snorts and snuffles. It did not shine at all in the room in which Olive slept, for the windows faced the other way. She slept uneasily, with her head under the bedclothes, as though fearful of what her eyes might see if she woke suddenly during the night, and she moaned fitfully. The moonlight came boldly into Colonel Bramber's room for the window was wide open and the curtains flung back. The Colonel liked to be awakened in the morning by the sun. Mrs. Bramber, in the adjoining room, slept with windows tightly shut and the curtains drawn, and slept remarkably soundly for an incurable invalid.

Only the faintest ray percolated into the room where Mr. Boggs lay in his lonely bed and dreamed of sirloins and topsides and luscious undercuts. To Peter Hunt the moonlight came in a softly diffused glow through diaphanous curtains as he slept deeply and refreshingly, and to his sister a little less brightly. It peeped curiously in at Mr. Penny, sleeping the sleep of the tired and the just and lingered softly in the room of Harriet Medcott, dreaming of the return of her husband. It visited at some time during the night, all the inhabitants of Long Manton. In Mrs. Withers's room it wasted little of its substance, flinging merely a brief and jagged patch upon the wall, but in Diana's room it was more generous, lying in a broad band across the foot of the bed. In Mr. Withers's room it was kept at bay by the light which was still on and under which he sat with furrowed brow and eyes smarting from lack of sleep, wondering how he could meet the bills which littered the table under his shaking hand.

The moon came at last to the window of Mrs. Mallaby's bedroom but here it was refused admittance by the blinds which fitted closely and kept out every vestige of light. In the big, luxurious bed she tossed and turned in the darkness, tormented by the rich food which her overburdened stomach was trying to digest, or perhaps by a premonition in her dreams that this was the last natural sleep she would ever have and that her next would be the sleep of eternity.

★ ★ ★

Peter was up early on the following morning. The two hours he had spent on his book on the previous night had been profitable and it was going well, and he was feeling all the joy which the creative artist feels when he is doing good work.

After an uncertain period, during which he had rewritten the opening five times, he had at last got what he wanted. Getting the thing started was always the more difficult part of the job. Once the first forty or fifty pages were written he could usually go happily along until the book was completed with, perhaps, one or two hold-ups if he came up against a knotty problem in the working out of the plot.

And such a situation developed after lunch that day.

After working rapidly and well all the morning, he had looked forward to continuing during the afternoon, but he had scarcely settled down again at his desk before he came up against a snag.

Leaning back in his chair he lighted a cigarette, hoping that the snag would yield to a little thought and tobacco.

But it did not.

It merely gave birth to another and even worse snag, so that at the end of half an hour he had two instead of one to deal with.

He wrestled with the problem for over an hour and a half without gaining any headway, and at last decided there was only one way of tackling the situation: put the whole thing out of his mind and let his subconscious deal with it in its own good time.

He decided to go for a walk.

There had been no break in the weather, if anything it was hotter than the previous day, and he took the path through the woods that would bring him out by the old church and so round through the village and back home.

It was a quarter to four when he left his house and he calculated that he could be home again by five, in time for tea.

Resolutely refusing to allow his mind to dwell on his problem, for he knew by past experience that that was fatal, Peter set out on his walk. The footpath through the woods came out into a lane and, eventually, to the Green and the High Street.

The clock in the tower of St. Mary's Church struck the half-hour as he reached the Green and struck across it towards the bottom of the High Street. So far the subconscious had not acted up to its reputation. Nothing in the nature of a solution had, as yet, come pushing its way up from those mysterious depths.

Peter was very disappointed in his subconscious.

But it couldn't be bullied into action. It had to take its own time to work things out in its own way, and it had never let him down in the past.

He called in to the little tobacconist's shop in the High Street and bought some cigarettes and then continued his way until he came to the church. The lovely old building always attracted him and he stopped to admire its architecture.

He was on the point of walking on again when Mr. Billing, the verger, suddenly shot out of the main door as though he had been propelled from an unseen catapult, and came running towards him.

'Mr. Hunt . . . Mr. Hunt . . . ' he called in a husky voice. 'Mr. Hunt . . . '

His florid face was a pasty grey and he was waving his arms jerkily.

Peter stopped in astonishement. Mr. Billing was usually a most phlegmatic man. What on earth could be the matter with him?

'What's the matter, Billing?' he asked, but the verger was for the moment breathless and inarticulate.

'What's the matter?' asked Peter again.

'Mrs. Mallaby . . . ' panted the verger, 'Mrs. Mallaby . . . '

'What's the matter with Mrs. Mallaby?' demanded Peter.

'There's something the matter with 'er,' gasped the verger. 'She's ill . . . She won't move . . . I touched her an' she won't move . . . ' Mr. Billing was almost incoherent. 'She won't move . . . There's blood on her . . . '

He held up a shaking hand and Peter saw, with a sudden catch of his breath, that it was smeared red . . .

'I'll come and see,' he said quickly, and ran up the path to the main door of the church with the verger at his heels. It was very dim inside except for the great west window which flamed with colour and splashed the lovely carving of the rood-screen with blue and red and orange. In a pew near the pulpit, Peter saw a dark figure, kneeling motionless as though in prayer . . .

'There she is,' whispered the scared Mr. Billing with a quiver in his voice. 'There she is . . . over there . . . '

Peter went over to the motionless form and leaned forward.

Mrs. Mallaby was kneeling on a hassock, her elbows resting on the narrow shelf provided for hymn books in front of her. Her face was covered by her hands, and her head, swathed in a black silk turban, was bent forward devoutly, exposing the nape of her neck. The skin was sunburned, and just below the hair was a small slit-like wound from which a trickle of blood had oozed and run down her neck, staining the white collar of her blouse.

Peter stared at the blood in horrified amazement while the verger breathed heavily and nasally over his shoulder. Then he reached forward and touched the kneeling woman on the arm.

There was no reaction. She remained motionless.

He turned quickly to Mr. Billing.

'You'd better get hold of Doctor Pratt at once,' he said urgently. 'I think she's dead.'

The breath whistled in the verger's throat as he drew it in sharply.

'Dead?' he repeated rather stupidly.

Peter nodded.

'Yes,' he said curtly, with his eyes fixed on the back of Mrs. Mallaby's neck. 'And when you've got the doctor you'd better get the police. I believe she's been murdered.'

3

The flame of the west window had died away and a cluster of gas jets had been lighted to chase away the gloom in the immediate vicinity of the pew in which the dead woman still knelt.

Police Constable Rutt, looking a little nervous and out of his depth, but striving valiantly to maintain the dignity of the law, stood, notebook in hand, solemnly sucking a pencil, while Doctor Pratt bent over the dead woman and made his examination.

Outside the circle of light thrown by the gas cluster, Peter and Mr. Billing watched in silence. The Reverend Mr. Popkiss, his flabby face whiter than usual, stood by the pulpit, peering through his glasses with a look of fascinated horror.

Rutt and the doctor had arrived together. The verger, on his way to the doctor, had met the constable crossing the Green and had hurriedly told him what had happened. Rutt, suddenly confronted with the possibility of a murder case, and a little doubtful about his ability to handle it, had, very sensibly, telephoned to the police station at Wincaster, the nearest town, for assistance. A superintendent and a detective sergeant were on their way. In the meantime, Rutt had been instructed to see that nothing was disturbed and that the church was closed.

Doctor Pratt straightened up, took off his glasses, polished them on his handkerchief, and put them on again.

'She is quite dead,' he announced briefly.

'What was the cause of death, doctor?' asked Rutt, preparing to note down the answer.

'The base of the brain has been pierced by a small, sharp instrument,' replied Doctor Pratt. 'Death would have been almost instantaneous — a matter of only a few seconds at the most.'

'Could she 'ave done it 'erself?' asked Rutt, after he had laboriously written down the reply to his first question.

The little doctor shook his head decisively.

'Quite impossible,' he declared. 'The angle of penetration, and the position in which she was found, discount any such possibility.'

So it *was* murder, thought Peter. He had expected no other answer, but the confirmation was, nevertheless, a shock. This would give the village something to talk about with a vengeance. Who among that small community was responsible for this?

Mr. Billing was giving an account of his discovery, and Peter listened.

It was, he said, his custom to visit the church at half-past four to see that everything was in order. This afternoon he had arrived as usual and seen Mrs. Mallaby, as he thought, praying. He was not surprised because she always came to pray for a minute or two every afternoon about that time, but she was generally gone before he put in an appearance. He had busied himself quietly about the chancel, expecting that she would shortly get up and go. After some time, seeing that she still remained motionless, in the same position, he had thought that she might, possibly, have fallen asleep. Rather hesitantly he had approached her and called her softly by name. When this had no effect he had laid his hand on her shoulder. His fingers had come in contact with something that was sticky and he had then seen, to his horror, that there was blood on the back of her neck. He had rushed out of the church with the intention of calling the vicar, but had encountered Mr. Hunt at the gate and he had accompanied him back.

Peter confirmed this part of his statement and added his own meagre offering of information, all of which Constable Rutt, with a portentous frown and much difficulty, transferred to the black notebook.

The Reverend Mr. Popkiss, who had throughout all this remained in a dazed silence, now felt it incumbent upon himself to make some suitable comment.

'It is indeed terrible — terrible,' he said in a hushed voice. 'A wicked and dreadful deed. I trust that the perpetrator of this evil thing will quickly be brought to justice.'

'The law will take care o' that,' said Rutt with great dignity. And at that moment there was a loud knocking that echoed through the empty church. 'That'll be the Sup'ntendent from Wincaster,' added the constable, and he went majestically to open the door.

★ ★ ★

Superintendent Hockley was a man of medium height with shrewd, humorous eyes and thinnish hair that was going grey at the sides. His manner was quiet and almost deferential, but it was possible to sense the authority that lurked behind this outward display of amiability.

Peter liked the look of him but decided that he would be a very unpleasant customer to come up against.

He had brought with him a detective sergeant, a photographer, and a fingerprint expert and also the police doctor. He listened without interruption while Rutt related the circumstances in which the crime had been discovered, and then, having heard what Doctor Pratt had to say regarding the cause of death, he began his own investigation.

The police doctor, a stout, bald-headed man, with a face like a cherub, examined the body and confirmed Doctor Pratt's statement. Death had taken place within the last three hours; he could not be more definite than that.

'Can you suggest the type of weapon?' asked Hockley.

'Something narrow and sharp — on the thin side, too,' said the police doctor. 'A penknife or something similar would have done the trick. Don't you agree?' He glanced politely at Doctor Pratt, who nodded in agreement.

'A penknife, eh?' said the superintendent thoughtfully. 'H'm, well, thank you, doctor.' He beckoned to the photographer. 'Now,' he continued briskly, 'before we go any further I'd like some photographs. I want four close-ups of the body from here, and here, and from here and here,' rapidly he pointed out the positions from which he wished the photographs taken, 'and a long shot from the door over there.'

The photographer had already unpacked his apparatus and for the next few minutes was busy filling the church with the glare of flash-bulbs.

When the photographs had been attended to, Hockley put on a pair of cotton gloves and made a close inspection of the body, the pew and the other pews in the immediate vicinity, paying particular attention to the pew directly behind Mrs. Mallaby. He finished his examination and called the fingerprint man forward.

'Come and see what you can find,' he said. 'You'd better bring out all the prints you can, especially on that rounded wooden piece directly behind, and on either side of, the body. When you've brought 'em out, Smollet can photograph 'em. When he's done, Sergeant, you can arrange for the removal of the body.' He turned and addressed the Reverend Mr. Popkiss. 'I should be glad, sir,' he said, 'if you would tell me where I can conduct this inquiry. The church seems hardly suitable. Perhaps there's a room of some sort . . . '

The vicar pursed his thick lips.

'Ah, yes,' he said, 'a — ah — room. Now let me see . . . The — ah — vestry, perhaps . . . '

'The very thing, sir,' agreed Hockley.

'You won't want me any more, will you?' asked the police doctor. 'I'll let you have a report after the post-mortem.'

'No, that's all right,' said Hockley.

'I should like to get away, too,' put in Doctor Pratt. 'I was in the middle of my tea . . . '

'Yes, there's nothing more you can do,' interrupted the superintendent. 'The dead woman was, I take it, a patient of yours?'

'If you can call it that,' said Doctor Pratt with a faint smile. 'The only thing I ever treated her for was a common cold. For a woman who persistently over-ate she had a remarkable constitution.'

He left in company with the police doctor, and when they had gone Hockley asked to be taken to the vestry, where he made himself comfortable at a small table. Producing a notebook and pencil, he laid them in front of himself, frowned thoughtfully, and looked up at Mr. Billing.

'Now,' he began, clearing his throat. 'I should like to get this right, if you don't mind.' He ran over Rutt's account of how the discovery had been made. 'Is that correct?'

Mr. Billing, who had recovered a little of his usual deliberation, agreed that it was quite correct.

'Can you tell me the exact time you entered the church this afternoon?' continued Hockley.

'At twenty minutes to five,' said the verger promptly. 'I always look up at the clock in the tower when I enter the gate.'

'I see. Do you come to the church every afternoon at that time?'

'Within a few minutes or so either way.'

'Is the church always open?'

'Yes.'

'And you always come in by the main door?'

'Yes. That's the only one left open. The other doors are all locked.'

'When you arrived this afternoon was there anybody else in the church except yourself and the deceased?'

'I didn't see anyone.'

'But it would be possible, wouldn't it, for someone to have been there without you seeing them?'

Mr. Billing considered this carefully before he replied.

'You mean if they was hiding?' he asked, and the superintendent nodded. 'Well, yes, I suppose it would have been possible,' said the verger doubtfully, as though such a thing was not very likely.

Superintendent Hockley did not press the point further.

'Were you surprised to find the dead woman there?' he asked.

'I was surprised to find her there so late. Her usual time was round about four.'

'Her usual time?' Hockley raised his eyebrows in faint surprise. 'Was she in the habit of coming to the church every afternoon?'

'Yes. She used to drop in to pray.'

'Always at the same time?'

'Nearly always. She used to come in so that she could get back 'ome in time for her tea. She had that at half past four as a rule.'

The superintendent scratched his chin gently.

'Was this habit of hers generally known?' he said.

'Oh yes. I think most people round these parts knew about it.'

'Did anyone else have a similar habit of dropping into the church during the afternoon?'

'Not regular, like Mrs. Mallaby. Miss Dewsnap and Miss Ginch used to come sometimes, but they weren't regular.'

'So anybody who knew of this habit of the dead woman's,' remarked the superintendent thoughtfully, 'would stand a very good chance of finding her quite alone in the church any afternoon between, say, a quarter to four and half past?'

'More often than not — yes.'

Hockley frowned at the note he had made, and there was a brief pause before he put his next question.

'Do you know of anyone who bore this

woman a sufficient grudge to want to kill her?' he asked suddenly.

Mr. Billing hesitated. Peter thought it was a very difficult question indeed to answer.

'Quite a lot of people didn't like her,' said the verger at length, skating round the difficulty diplomatically. 'But I couldn't think of anyone who'd want her dead.'

'Somebody did,' said Superintendent Hockley. 'And whoever it was must've had a pretty good motive.' His shrewd eyes flickered from one to the other. 'What sort of a woman was she?' he asked.

The Reverend Mr. Popkiss, to whom the question had been addressed, gave a slight cough before he replied.

'She was a — ah — woman of very strong character,' he said. 'Very strong indeed. A devout Christian. It is dreadful that she should have been struck down — ah — while in the act of prayer. The villain responsible for this foul deed must be . . .'

'Quite, sir,' interrupted Hockley firmly.

'Can you suggest who the person might be?'

'I?' exclaimed Mr. Popkiss in consternation at the very idea. 'Good gracious, no. I have no idea in the least — in the least . . . '

'I only wondered if there was anyone you might suspect,' said Hockley. 'As vicar of the parish, you naturally know a great deal of what goes on . . . '

'It would make me very unhappy to think that it could be anyone known to me,' said the vicar, shaking his head sadly. 'I cannot believe such a thing to be possible.'

'I appreciate that, sir,' said the superintendent with the faintest touch of impatience in his voice. 'But you must understand that a murder has been committed by someone who was obviously aware of the dead woman's habits and that would appear to be someone she was well known to. The relationship between the people of your parish and the deceased is something that you know better than I. You know most of 'em intimately, I don't. Has there been any trouble with any particular person? Who were the people who disliked her and why? A hint might give me a line and save me a lot of valuable time.'

Mr. Popkiss shook his head slowly.

'I'm afraid I can't help you,' he replied gently. 'Mrs. Mallaby may have had enemies — who among us can say we have not? — but I know of no such hatred as would lead to murder.'

If Hockley was disappointed at this answer no sign of it appeared in his face. He went on to inquire about Mrs. Mallaby's history. What was her position? Had she had any relatives? Who had been her personal friends? A long list of questions that Peter thought seemed quite irrelevant to the inquiry. The vicar answered as many of them as he was able and, to Peter's surprise, seemed to know less about the dead woman than might have been expected.

When Hockley had exhausted the Reverend Mr. Popkiss he turned to Peter and began all over again. Halfway through the long inquisition, the sergeant — whose name it appeared was Twist

— put in a brief appearance to say that the photographer and the fingerprint expert had gone, and that the body had been removed. Hockley wrote something on a leaf of his notebook, tore it out, and handed it to his subordinate, who glanced at it, nodded, and went away again.

The examination then continued. It was rather amazing the number of questions that the superintendent thought of. He worried at a thing until he had squeezed every ounce of information out of it. There were, thought Peter with admiration, no flies on Superintendent Hockley. He was a man who obviously knew his job.

'Well, gentlemen,' he said at last, pocketing his notebook and getting up from the table. 'I think that will be all for the present. I may want to question you later in the light of any evidence that may come to hand. In the meanwhile, I should be glad if one of you would direct me to the dead woman's residence.'

Peter offered to set him on the right road and, after wishing the Reverend Mr. Popkiss and Mr. Billing goodbye, and informing the vicar that there was no reason to impose any restrictions on the use of the church, the superintendent left with him by the vestry door which the verger obligingly opened. The evening was beautiful, still and peaceful, and when the clock struck as they left the church, Peter was surprised to find that it was already a quarter to eight. His sister would be wondering what the dickens had happened to him, and he visualised her excited astonishment when she heard the news.

'Well, Mr. Hunt,' remarked the superintendent, producing a pipe and beginning to fill it from a shabby pouch, 'I suppose this is your first experience of murder, eh?'

Peter was a little startled for the moment, and then he realised what the other meant. He admitted that it was.

'We don't get many murders round these parts,' continued Hockley conversationally. 'Which is something to be thankful for. This is a queer business. I don't recollect ever hearing of a murder in a church before.'

They turned out of the High Street and into the foot-path that formed a short cut to Mrs. Mallaby's house.

'I'll show you where you go when we get to the end of this,' said Peter, and the superintendent was grateful.

'Thank you, sir,' he said. 'My sergeant has taken the car and gone on ahead to prepare the ground, so to speak.' He lit his pipe carefully and puffed at it with evident enjoyment. 'I hope I'm not taking you out of your way?'

'No, I can get home this way quite easily,' said Peter. 'It only makes a few minutes' difference. I must admit I'm interested. I've read about murder investigations, but this is the first I've actually seen in practice.'

'I'm afraid you'll find it a bit disappointing, sir,' said Hockley. 'It's mostly a question of asking this, that and the other an' piecing the answers together until you get some sort of a pattern.' He shook his head. 'Not much excitement, like you read about in books. Just patience an' plodding. Weary work most of it.'

'In this particular case,' said Peter, 'you can surely weed out quite a number of people who couldn't have done it. The murder must have been committed between the time Mrs. Mallaby entered the church and the time Billing arrived there. All the people who can provide an alibi for that period can be wiped off your list of suspects.'

'That's right, sir,' agreed Hockley.

'Of those that remain you've got to find the one with the strongest motive and you've got your murderer.'

Superintendent Hockley chuckled softly.

'It sounds all right, Mr. Hunt,' he said. 'But it doesn't work out as easily as that. For one thing, how many people do you suppose will be able to supply an alibi for that particular time? Not as many as you'd think, I'll be bound. An' then so far as the remainder are concerned, it's not always the strongest motive that results in a crime of this sort. A man once murdered his wife because she would keep sniffing instead of blowing her nose, an' it got on his nerves. Besides, from what I can gather, there seem to be plenty o' people hereabouts with a motive of one sort or another. The dead woman was not exactly popular, was she?'

'That is putting it mildly,' said Peter.

'You see what I mean, sir?' went on Hockley. 'What you or I might not consider a strong enough motive for murder might appear very different to the murderer. It's a question of the outlook. There's a lot in what you say, all the same,' added the superintendent kindly.

They came to the end of the narrow path and out into the road beyond.

'Manton Lodge is just round the bend on the right,' said Peter. 'You can't miss it. I go this way,' he pointed to where the path continued through a small copse on the other side of the road.

'Thank you, sir,' said Hockley. 'I'm very much obliged to you. I take it, if there's anything further I want to ask you, you won't object to me calling . . . '

'Only too glad,' said Peter. 'I'd like to know how things progress, if you can spare the time.'

'I dare say I can manage to do that, sir,'

said Hockley. 'Good night, sir.'

'Good night.'

Peter crossed the road and was lost among the trees, and the superintendent, drawing thoughtfully on his pipe, continued slowly on his way to Manton Lodge.

He foresaw a difficult job ahead of him, but the hunt was up and sooner or later, they would come to the kill.

4

Long Manton, as a whole, received the news of the murder with shocked surprise and excitement, and individually with mixed feelings.

Miss Ginch, the late Mrs. Mallaby's most intimate friend, was so overcome with grief that she took to her bed with a bottle of smelling salts and a prayer book, and, between intervals of sniffing and reading the burial service, wondered if the dead woman had left her any practical token of her affection in her will. Miss Dewsnap, unable to go to this extreme on account of her duties in the post office, contented herself by raising her eyes to heaven at every mention of Mrs. Mallaby's name, as though she expected to see that large lady, robed diaphanously and complete with halo, descend through the ceiling on a cloud.

Mrs. Conway remarked caustically that 'she only got what she deserved,' and Mr.

Boggs shrugged his broad shoulders and said: 'Well, it'll be no good grumbling about the meat where *she's* gone to.'

Mrs. Withers and Diana discussed the matter between themselves, and with anybody else who would listen, treating it as though it were something that had happened in a book, and speculating on who could have done it and why. Mr. Withers appeared chiefly concerned from a business point of view, and the effect it would have on the large account which the bank carried.

Mrs. Bramber, suffering from a worse attack of her mysterious complaint than usual, demanded all the news, with an avid interest that surprised her husband and kept him constantly on the go between Pondicherry Cottage and the village in an attempt to keep his wife supplied with the latest developments.

The Reverend Mr. Popkiss spoke unctuously of the 'dear departed lady' and shook his head sorrowfully as though he was not quite sure where she had departed to.

The Fox and Hounds became the centre of a group of amateur detectives who evolved all kinds of theories and suggested all kinds of motives, and argued heatedly about How, Who, Why and When, and involved nearly everybody in Long Manton except those who happened to be present in the bar at that particular time.

The comings and goings of Superintendent Hockley and his subordinates were watched with great interest, and the sudden descent of a contingent of newspaper reporters, who arrived out of nowhere, like one of the plagues of Egypt, caused another mild sensation.

They swarmed over the village, took photographs of the church, both inside and out, questioned everybody who had even remotely known the dead woman, and generally made themselves a nuisance, to the annoyance of Hockley and the majority of the villagers.

Peter came in for a great deal of their attention. He was already 'news' to a certain extent and, coupled with the murder, was good 'copy.' The enterprising editor of one well-known daily even telephoned suggesting that Peter should 'cover' the murder for his paper. He refused the offer, but the suggestion gave him an idea. He was intensely interested in the murder, and he had lived in the village long enough to know something of its people and their queer psychology. Why shouldn't he, for his own amusement, have a shot at solving the mystery?

It appealed to him so much that he went in search of his sister then and there, found her in the kitchen making cakes, and told her what he had decided.

She laughed sceptically. 'What do you know about detection?' she demanded. 'You don't even write detective stories.'

Peter was not to be put off by her lack of faith in him.

'You just wait and see,' he retorted.

'I will,' replied Margaret derisively. 'When are you going to begin?'

'Now,' said Peter, and left it at that.

* * *

Superintendent Hockley had been a very busy man during the time that had elapsed since the discovery of the murder, and he had, as a result of his efforts, acquired a considerable amount of useful information. From Mrs. Gener, the housekeeper at Manton Lodge, he learned that on the afternoon of her death Mrs. Mallaby had left the house at five minutes to four with the intention of visiting the church for her usual daily interlude of prayer. She had informed the parlourmaid, as she went out, that she would be back at twenty minutes past four and that she would require her tea, as usual, at half past.

Mrs. Mallaby had been very punctilious regarding time and when she had not returned as she said she would, Mrs. Gener had been very surprised but she had not been worried. She thought that perhaps her mistress had met someone and been detained.

The housekeeper's story was confirmed by the parlourmaid and the cook. This information was of the utmost importance because it narrowed down the time element considerably.

If the dead woman had contemplated returning home by twenty past four, it was only reasonable to suppose that she must have been dead at that hour, since, if she had been alive, she would surely have left the church. It took five minutes, roughly, to reach the church from Manton Lodge, so if she had gone straight there, as she had said, she would have arrived at the church at four o'clock or a minute or so after that hour. This allowed a period of fifteen minutes during which the murder must have been committed. Or so it seemed.

Even supposing that she had stayed longer than she had intended this could not have been for more than a few minutes, for at twenty-five minutes to five Mr. Billing had arrived and she was already dead.

It seemed that it was fairly safe to conclude that she had come by her death between five minutes past four and half past four.

This, of course, was always supposing that Mr. Billing himself was not the murderer, a contingency that Hockley did not fail to take into account.

The superintendent was very well satisfied at having been able to limit the time to such a short period. It was going to be a great help when he reached the stage of sifting out any possible suspects. Just at present he was more interested in collecting everything he could concerning the dead woman.

Having learned all he could from the housekeeper, which was disappointingly little, he conducted a careful search of Mrs. Mallaby's personal possessions. In the desk in the corner of the drawing-room, which he opened with the keys that Sergeant Tripp had taken from the dead woman's handbag and brought with him, he discovered several letters from a firm of solicitors, all neatly bound together with a rubber band. The letters themselves were of no particular interest, they merely referred to property investments, but the name of the firm and its London address, embossed in shiny black at the head of the paper, was a different matter. If Messrs. Nodds, Buncombe, Nodds and

Buncombe had been the dead woman's regular solicitors, they might be able to suggest a possible motive for her death and, at any rate, should be informed of it at once.

Hockley made a careful note of the address and telephone number and turned his attention to the other contents of the desk.

There were a number of receipted bills and several unpaid ones. Other than those from the solicitors there were no other letters at all. Hockley thought that this was rather unusual, but concluded that Mrs. Mallaby had been one of those people who destroyed all correspondence except business matters as soon as answered.

He came upon a cheque book in a narrow drawer, together with a passbook and a small bundle of cancelled cheques. The amount of the balance shown in the passbook made him purse up his lips in a silent whistle. He had been unprepared to discover how very well off the dead woman had been.

In the light of this fresh knowledge, the

murder took on a different aspect. Perhaps here lay the motive?

She had been, apparently, without living relatives from what he had already gathered. In which case who got all the money now that she was dead? The solicitors would, mostly likely, be able to answer that. One of the first things he must do in the morning was to get in touch with them.

In the meanwhile, time was getting on and there was still a lot to be done. He had his report to write for the Chief Constable.

It wasn't much good theorising or speculating at this early stage. Collect all the facts first and start thinking about them afterwards was his motto. Otherwise you were apt to twist a few facts to make them fit a theory, and that was fatal . . .

The cheque-book stubs yielded nothing of importance. The cheques, of which they formed a record, had been mostly issued to local tradespeople in payment of accounts. The butcher, the baker, the grocer . . .

There was one to a big London store

for seventy-five pounds, ten shillings and sevenpence, and two or three to self for varying amounts. That was all.

Hockley made a mental note to interview the bank manager on the morrow. He would have a pretty full day it seemed. There was the coroner to see and arrange about the inquest, the solicitors to telephone, the bank manager to see, and he would have to have a word with the Chief Constable . . . Yes, a pretty full day.

And he still had that infernal report to write that night.

Better call it a day. Oh, well, he hadn't done so badly for a beginning — he couldn't feel any grass growing under his feet, anyway . . . That fellow, Hunt, was a nice chap — might prove to be a bit helpful, too. Had his head screwed on the right way. The missus had had one of his books out of the library the other week and said she liked it. *He* never got much time for reading . . .

With the assistance of Sergeant Tripp, a large and taciturn man who had made a thorough search of the rest of the house without finding anything important, Superintendent Hockley packed up the contents of the desk into a neat parcel, relocked it, and departed in his car to Wincaster to write the report for the Chief Constable and, afterwards, seek what rest he could to fit him for the busy day to come.

★ ★ ★

The telephone call which Hockley put through at nine-thirty on the following morning to Messrs. Nodds, Buncombe, Nodds and Buncombe, caused much the same result as might an explosion of a bomb in that old-fashioned firm of solicitors. The call was passed on at once to the only living Mr. Buncombe himself, who in a brittle, high-pitched voice, demanded to know the full details, and announced his intention of coming down by the first available train.

Since the first available train could not get him to Wincaster before noon, and he then had to find a form of conveyance to transport him the thirty-odd miles to

Long Manton — there was only one bus which did the journey twice daily — Hockley concluded that it was unlikely he would have the pleasure of meeting Mr. Buncombe much before two o'clock in the afternoon.

He had the morning free, therefore, to attend to the other jobs he had set himself.

He paid a visit to the Coroner and arranged for the inquest to be held in the village schoolroom — a fact that was hailed by all the children with joy because it meant an unexpected holiday — at eleven o'clock on the Monday morning. The police doctor's report of the post-mortem had been left for him and a copy of this was left with the Coroner for his especial information.

Hockley was anxious that the inquest should not be a protracted affair. Evidence of identification, and the cause of death, was all that was necessary, and then an adjournment for a fortnight. That would give him time to marshal his facts into a more or less coherent pattern.

The Coroner was, luckily, a reasonable

man who saw Hockley's point of view and agreed with it.

Relieved that this had been attended to satisfactorily, the superintendent drove over to Long Manton, called at the United Capital Bank and sought an interview with the manager.

Mr. Withers, looking as worried and harassed as usual, invited him into his office and nervously offered him a chair.

'Thank you, sir,' said Hockley, sitting down. 'I'm sorry to have to trouble you like this.'

'Don't m-mention it,' said Mr. Withers, blinking at him. 'I rather expected a visit from you, Superintendent.'

'Did you, sir?' remarked Hockley amiably. 'Well, now that makes it a bit easier. I should be glad of any information you can give me concerning the late Mrs. Mallaby which might have a bearing on her death.'

'A terrible thing. Most unfortunate,' murmured Mr. Withers, playing with a pencil on his desk. 'I d-don't see quite how I can help you, Superintendent.'

'Well, sir,' said Hockley smoothly,

wondering how such a nervous little man could ever have become a bank manager, 'I'd just like to get the financial side of the business straight. Make certain there's nothing irregular, if you understand what I mean?'

Mr. Withers nodded gently.

'I found a passbook, a partly used cheque book, and a lot of cancelled cheques at Manton Lodge, and I'd like to check them over with you, if you'd be so kind.'

He produced from a small attaché case the things he had mentioned and laid them carefully on the desk. Mr. Withers, with his usual worried frown that had grown into a permanency from long habit, went methodically through the cheques, comparing them with the passbook.

'These appear to be quite in order,' he said at length. 'Of course the credit balance shown here is n-not quite right. This passbook was m-made up to the end of last month and there have been several cheques issued since, including the one for five hundred pounds.'

Hockley pricked up his ears.

'Which one was that, sir?' he inquired with sudden interest

'It was a cheque Mrs. M-Mallaby cashed herself over the counter,' explained Mr. Withers. 'Last Monday. It was made out to self.'

Hockley picked up the cheque book and looked through the stubs rapidly.

'There's nothing here, sir,' he said.

'There wouldn't be,' answered Mr. Withers. 'She had left her cheque book behind. I gave her a separate cheque form.'

'Oh, I see, sir,' said the superintendent.

'She wrote out the cheque and I gave her cash for it,' continued the bank manager.

Hockley pursed his lips and gently scratched his chin.

'Was she in the habit of drawing out such large sums in cash, sir?' he asked.

Mr. Withers shook his head.

'N-no,' he answered. 'She had never done such a thing before.'

'You've no idea what she wanted it for?' asked Hockley.

'No. I concluded from her manner that it was for s-something urgent. She wished for the money in pound notes . . . '

'In pound notes?' said Hockley sharply.

'Yes, she insisted on that,' said the bank manager. 'I can't imagine why. Five-pound notes would have been much more convenient. The amount in pounds was rather b-bulky.'

'Didn't you think it rather strange, sir?' said Hockley.

'Yes, I did,' admitted Mr. Withers. 'But Mrs. Mallaby was not an easy woman to question. It was really none of my business, you see.'

'Quite so, sir,' agreed the superintendent. 'Have you the cheque?'

'Yes, of course,' said Mr. Withers. 'You would like to see it, I suppose?'

'If you please, sir,' said Hockley.

Mr. Withers pressed a bell on his desk, and in a few minutes a tall, lanky, round-shouldered man slouched in.

'Oh — er — Mr. Totts,' said Mr. Withers diffidently. 'That cheque we cashed for Mrs. M-Mallaby last Monday. Would you let me have it please?'

'Yes, sir,' said Mr. Totts, who was the cashier, and the only other member of the staff except for a junior clerk, in a deep and sepulchral voice. He went out and was gone for a matter of only two or three seconds. When he came back he was carrying a slip of pink paper which he laid on the desk in front of Mr. Withers.

'Is that all, sir?' he asked in a tone that implied he thought it was quite sufficient for one morning's work.

'Yes, thank you,' said the bank manager, and the ungainly figure of Mr. Totts shuffled out of the office.

Mr. Withers picked up the cheque delicately, looked at it with a worried frown, and handed it to the superintendent. Hockley took it and inspected it carefully.

There was no mistaking Mrs. Mallaby's bold writing. The cheque was made payable to 'cash' and therefore required no endorsement.

'And you have no idea at all what this money could have been for, sir?' asked Hockley.

'None whatever,' declared Mr. Withers.

'I rather wondered at the t-time.'

'Would you have any objection to my keeping this cheque, sir?' said the superintendent. 'I'll give you an official receipt for it, of course.'

Mr. Withers looked doubtful.

'It's rather irregular,' he demurred. 'But I suppose in the circumstances . . . '

'Thank you, sir,' broke in Hockley and he put the cheque away in his pocket-book. He wrote out a receipt and rose to take his leave.

'I'm very much obliged to you, sir,' he said. 'What you've told me may be of very great help.'

Here was something, he thought, as he walked up the High Street, watched curiously by the villagers who happened to be in the vicinity, that wanted a lot of thinking over. Why had the dead woman drawn out that large sum of money in one-pound notes? What had become of it? There had been no trace of it at her house. If it had been necessary for her to pay away such a large sum, why hadn't she paid it by cheque, or if cash was essential, why not in notes of a higher denomination which would have been less bulky? The obvious answer to that was that pound notes were difficult to trace. If that was her reason it was rather queer. The ominous word 'blackmail' hovered uncertainly in Hockley's mind as he walked across the Green.

That might be it. If so, what then? Who could have been blackmailing Mrs. Mallaby and why? Maybe Mr. Buncombe would know something about that five hundred pounds when he arrived that afternoon. Then again, maybe he wouldn't.

★　★　★

Mr. Nathaniel Buncombe arrived at Manton Lodge in a hired car just after two. He was a very large, very red-faced, very bald man, with a very large stomach artistically draped with a very large gold watch chain. Everything about Mr. Buncombe was very large. The two gold rings on his chubby fingers that had sunk so far into the flesh that they would never come off; the gold pin with the onyx centre in his black cravat; the gold cuff-links in his immaculate stiff shirt cuffs.

He dominated any room in which he happened to be, and he dominated the drawing-room at Manton Lodge as he stood in front of the fire and surveyed Superintendent Hockley through a pair of gold-rimmed spectacles with his hands clasped behind his very large back.

The superintendent, seated at a small table, had just finished an account of the murder, to which the solicitor had listened with the closest attention and without interruption.

Now that Hockley had concluded, he took off his glasses and polished them vigorously with a large silk handkerchief.

'Very distressing — very distressing indeed,' he remarked. 'I am amazed and grieved to hear that such a terrible thing should have happened to a — er — client of ours.'

He gave the impression that other, and less exalted solicitors had clients that were being constantly murdered, but not a reputable firm like Nodds, Buncombe,

Nodds and Buncombe.

'Yes, sir,' murmured Hockley noncommittally.

'How far have your investigations progressed towards apprehending the murderer?' asked Mr. Buncombe, holding his spectacles up to the light and peering carefully through each lens in turn.

'Not very far at present, I'm afraid, sir,' answered the superintendent.

'You have no suspicion as to who could have been guilty of this appalling crime?' asked the lawyer, his eyebrows ascending slightly, as though he were rather surprised that Hockley had not already got the culprit under lock and key.

'No, sir. I haven't got as far as suspicions of anybody yet,' said the superintendent. 'I lack quite a lot of information regarding the deceased which might be of assistance to me. I'm hoping you may be able to help me there, sir.'

Mr. Buncombe replaced his spectacles and looked over the tops of them.

'What do you wish to know?' he inquired.

'Everything about Mrs. Mallaby that

you can tell me, sir,' answered Hockley promptly. 'I want to get some idea of her background. At present I know very little.'

Mr. Buncombe considered this for some time in silence. Then he cleared his throat and said:

'Up to the time she married Mr. Mallaby, I know very little about her myself. She was a Miss Horton. Mr. Mallaby was our client and when he married, of course, his wife became our client too. She was an extremely able businesswoman.'

'Mr. Mallaby, I take it, was a very rich man?' said Hockley.

'Very rich — very rich indeed.' Mr. Buncombe nodded several times to show that there was no doubt about *that*. ' 'Mallaby's Purgative Pills,' you know. He amassed a huge fortune from the business which he afterwards sold — at his wife's request, I believe.'

'She inherited all the money?' asked Hockley.

'Yes, with the exception of a few small bequests to friends,' answered Mr. Buncombe. 'He was without other kith or kin.'

'Was it a large amount?'

'A little over seven hundred thousand pounds,' said Mr. Buncombe, lowering his voice in deference to such a large sum of money. 'Of course there were death duties, but the widow received quite a respectable sum — quite a respectable sum.'

'Who will benefit by that now?' asked Hockley.

For the first time Mr. Buncombe looked distressed.

'There was no will,' he said shaking his head sorrowfully. 'Unless there is some next of kin of whom I am not aware, the estate will go to the Crown.'

'Isn't it a little strange that Mrs. Mallaby left no will?' said Hockley in surprise.

'I was constantly urging her to do so,' said Mr. Buncombe. 'There are, you know, some people who are very reluctant to do so. They fight shy of all — er — idea of death. I think Mrs. Mallaby was in that category.'

But death had come all the same — suddenly and unexpectedly.

'Do you know of anyone,' said Hockley, 'to whom she has recently paid the sum of five hundred pounds in cash?'

Mr. Buncombe did not. The superintendent thereupon told him about the cheque which Mrs. Mallaby had cashed at the United Capital Bank on the Monday before she had been killed.

The solicitor was astonished.

'Extraordinary,' he remarked, frowning down at his highly polished shoes. 'Really most strange. I wonder why she could have required such a large sum in such small currency?'

'You know nothing about it then, sir?' said Hockley. 'I was hoping you might be able to tell me what had become of this money.'

'You have not been able to trace it?' inquired Mr. Buncombe.

Hockley shook his head.

'Really, *most* extraordinary,' said the lawyer, gently stroking his chin.

'I was wondering . . . ' began Hockley and hesitated.

'What?' prompted Mr. Buncombe.

'I was wondering, sir,' continued the

superintendent, 'if there could be anything that the deceased didn't wish to become known . . . something, perhaps, that someone knew and . . . '

'Blackmail?' broke in Mr. Buncombe with a shrewd glance at the other.

'Yes, sir.'

The lawyer pursed his lips and looked up at the ceiling.

'I should hardly think . . . Um . . . Of course, I can't speak with any certainty,' he said, 'but I hardly think so. Surely if this was blackmail there would have been other — er — payments?'

'Unless this was the first,' said Hockley.

'Quite, quite,' said Mr. Buncombe. 'There is that, of course. It is certainly a possibility that should be taken into consideration. I cannot suggest any reason for blackmail, but then, as I told you, I know nothing about Mrs. Mallaby's early life. It seems, however, that if it were anything connected with that period, the blackmailer has been rather a long time in taking action.'

They were interrupted at that moment by a tap on the door and the arrival of the housemaid who announced that Mr. Peter Hunt would like to see the superintendent.

'Who,' said Mr. Buncombe, 'is Mr. Peter Hunt?'

Hockley explained.

'I think I'd better see him, sir,' he concluded. 'He may have some information . . . '

'Certainly, certainly,' agreed Mr. Buncombe, 'ask the gentleman to step in.'

The housemaid departed, returning in a few seconds to usher in Peter.

He had expected to find Hockley alone, and the unexpected sight of the pompous and imposing Mr. Buncombe, blocking up the fireplace, rather disconcerted him.

The superintendent introduced them and then, turning to Peter, said in a business-like voice:

'Well, Mr. Hunt, what do you want to see me about?'

The directness of this question was even more disconcerting than the presence of the solicitor, since Peter had sought out Hockley for no other reason than because he wished to find out how the investigation was going.

'It was really nothing of great importance,' he said. 'I only came to see if I could be of any assistance to you.'

'That's very kind of you, sir,' said Hockley, and the faintest trace of a humorous twinkle showed in his eyes. 'I can't think of any way at the moment, but I'm much obliged all the same.'

'If I'd known you were engaged, I wouldn't have butted in,' said Peter apologetically.

'That's all right, Mr. Hunt,' said the superintendent. 'I appreciate your taking the trouble . . . '

Again there was an interruption by the housemaid.

'I'm very sorry, sir,' said the girl, 'but there's a lady wishes to see you.'

'Wants to see me?' repeated the superintendent.

'I s'pose so,' said the housemaid. 'She asked for the police officer in charge of the case . . . '

'What's her name? Who is she?' demanded the superintendent.

'You don't know me, and you wouldn't

know my name,' interrupted a clear, pleasant voice from the doorway.

A girl entered the room. She was tall, and dressed in a tailored suit of some black material that fitted her admirable figure without a wrinkle. A smart black hat was perched at exactly the right angle on her well-shaped head and enhanced the shining chestnut of her hair.

She looked from one to the other with a faint smile, and her attitude was one of complete self-assurance. Peter, who had never seen her before in his life, experienced a queer feeling of familiarity, and was puzzled to account for it. Whatever Hockley and Mr. Buncombe felt, their predominant sensation was one of utter astonishment. That was obvious from the expression on their faces.

They stared at the attractive visitor for a few seconds in complete silence, and then the solicitor found his voice.

'May I inquire, madam,' he said, pompously, 'who you are?'

'Certainly you may,' she answered coolly. 'I'm Mrs. Mallaby's illegitimate daughter!'

5

A deep hush fell on the room — a sudden, an awful silence. Mr. Buncombe's mouth drooped foolishly open so that he looked like a bespectacled codfish. Superintendent Hockley, with better control of his features, but not so perfect that his astonishment was not plainly visible, stared at the unperturbed utterer of this unexpected statement as though he were about to try a form of mild hypnotism. The housemaid gave vent to a stifled sound that was a mixture of gasp and giggle, grew very red in the face, and finally fled from the room.

Peter felt an irrepressible desire to laugh. It surged up within him, uncontrollable and quite impossible to check. He suddenly burst into a peal of laughter that shattered the silence like a stone hurled through a plate-glass window.

Mr. Buncombe started and glared at him in shocked disapproval. Hockley shifted his gaze from the girl to his polished boots. The visitor looked at Peter gravely, though there was a hint of amusement in her eyes.

'I appear,' she said, 'to have caused a sensation.'

Mr. Buncombe cleared his throat noisily. He grasped at a link of his massive gold watch-chain as though the touch of the solid metal afforded him a sense of material stability in this unprecedented situation.

'Would you be good enough to explain yourself?' he said, surveying the girl over the rims of his glasses.

'I thought I had made myself quite clear,' she answered, not in the least abashed.

Mr. Buncombe cleared his throat again.

'I hardly think this is an occasion for levity,' he said severely. 'Would you have the goodness, Mr. — er — Hunt, to stop that unseemly noise?'

Peter stifled his laughter with an effort.

'I beg your pardon,' he said huskily. 'I'm really very sorry.'

'Don't mind me,' said the girl calmly. 'I like to see people enjoy themselves.'

'I should be obliged,' said Mr. Buncombe, 'if you would kindly explain the meaning of your statement. Who are you?'

'I've already told you,' she answered. 'If you mean what is my name, I am known as Ann Lexford. That of course, is not my name because, legally, I have no name.' She looked at Mr. Buncombe. 'Now would you mind telling me who *you* are?'

Mr. Buncombe, with great dignity, informed her who he was.

'Oh, I see,' she said, quite unimpressed. 'You're the late Mrs. Mallaby's solicitor? Well, I'm the late Mrs. Mallaby's illegitimate daughter.' She smiled. 'You seem rather surprised.'

'I am most surprised,' said the lawyer. 'I had no idea . . . '

'I don't suppose you had,' she broke in. 'I don't think anyone knew. She wasn't, you know, very proud of the fact. I can assure you, however, that it's quite true. I have all the proof that you could wish.'

'Who — who was your father?' asked Mr. Buncombe.

The girl shook her head.

'I really haven't the slightest idea,' she replied. 'I can't say that I am very interested. It happened twenty-eight years ago, you see, when my mother was in service . . .'

'In service?' Mr. Buncombe's eyes nearly shot through the glass of his spectacles. 'Do you mean that she was — was a *servant*?'

'She was housemaid to some people called Harrington in Hampshire. Perhaps it would be better if I told you the whole story?'

Mr. Buncombe, for once completely bereft of speech, nodded.

'I'll sit down, if you don't mind,' she said. 'It's a little tiring standing.'

It was Peter who pushed forward a chair.

★　★　★

The story she told them, sitting there in the big drawing-room, was neither a very long, nor a very original one.

Julia Horton, as she was then, was not

90

the first to stray from the path of virtue and be sorry for it, and she would not be the last. She had got rid of her unwanted daughter as speedily as possible by finding a home for her with a Mrs. Cooper who undertook to look after the baby for ten shillings a week. Julia Horton had paid this sum regularly and washed her hands of her responsibility. A few years afterwards she married Mr. Mallaby and became a rich woman. She met him while she was on holiday at Weston-super-Mare and he had been quite unaware, when he had proposed to her, that she had ever been in service, or that she was the possessor of a daughter whose father was known to nobody but herself, and had remained unaware of it to the day of his death.

Ann had learned all this as a result of many and constant questions regarding her parentage to Mrs. Cooper as soon as she was old enough to be interested. She had, when she discovered the truth, wished, not unnaturally, to see her mother, but Mrs. Mallaby, now ensconced as the mistress of Manton

Lodge, and a respectable married woman, had refused either to meet or to have anything whatever to do with her.

She had, on her marriage, increased the amount to two pounds a week, and considered that she had done all that was necessary.

At the age of sixteen, Ann had taken the name of Lexford because she liked the sound of it, and got herself a job as junior typist with a firm of periodical publishers which specialised in women's magazines. When she had seen in the newspapers an account of the death of Mr. Mallaby, she had written at once to her mother, but the letter had been ignored and she had made no other attempt to communicate with her. At twenty-one she had become an assistant editor on one of the monthly magazines which her firm published. A year later she had been made editor and had shown such an aptitude for her work that she was now in control of a group of periodicals issued by the same firm.

She had continued to visit Mrs. Cooper, of whom she was very fond, but she had neither seen nor heard anything of her mother until that morning when she had seen in a newspaper that she was dead and that it was believed she had been murdered.

'The account in the paper was very brief,' she concluded, 'but I was anxious to know what had really happened, so I decided to come at once, and here I am.'

Mr. Buncombe expelled his breath slowly, took out a snowy handkerchief from his pocket and blew his nose violently.

'A most amazing story,' he remarked. 'I confess that I am — er — considerably astonished . . . '

'You shouldn't be,' said Ann. 'As a lawyer you should know that nearly everybody has something in their lives that they want to keep secret. In this case, I'm the skeleton in the cupboard.'

And a very attractive skeleton too, thought Peter.

'You say, miss,' said Superintendent Hockley, 'that you have proof of this — relationship with the deceased?'

'Oh, yes,' replied Ann. 'I have my birth

certificate. My mother's name appears on it as Julia Horton, spinster. Mrs. Cooper also has a number of letters which my mother wrote to her when I was a baby. I have the birth certificate with me.'

She opened her handbag and took out an envelope. It was Mr. Buncombe who took it from her and withdrew the folded paper it contained. Adjusting his spectacles, he glanced at it.

'This appears to be quite in order,' he said. 'It is, of course, a copy, but the original is easily available.'

She smiled at him sweetly.

'I think you will find the letters quite in order, too,' she said. 'Now, please, would you tell me exactly what happened?'

'Well, miss,' said Superintendent Hockley taking it upon himself to answer her. 'I'm afraid what we can tell you is very little. The murder was only discovered yesterday afternoon and there hasn't been much time . . . '

'It *was* murder, then?' said Ann. 'The paper I read said 'believed to have been murdered.''

'It was murder, right enough, miss,'

said Hockley. 'But we don't know yet who did it or why.'

'Tell me all you *do* know,' said the girl.

Hockley told her, with certain reservations. He said nothing about the cheque and the five hundred pounds in one-pound notes.

'It's rather — nasty, isn't it?' she commented, when he had finished. 'I mean the church — and while she was kneeling there . . . It — it makes it rather — horrible . . . '

The superintendent nodded.

'I suppose it does,' he said. He hesitated for a moment and then he continued: 'Had you any other reason, miss, for coming here this afternoon?'

She looked at him and her eyes twinkled.

'I had nothing to do with my mother's murder, if that's what you're thinking,' she said. 'I was in my office in London all yesterday afternoon, and at least thirty people can vouch for it.'

Hockley reddened slightly.

'I wasn't . . . ' he began.

'I came,' she went on, as though he

hadn't spoken, 'because I wanted to know. There was no sentiment about it. There is no sentiment about it. But she was my mother, and I want to know the truth about her death.'

At least, thought Peter, she's honest. She's not pretending to a feeling that she hasn't got, because it's the right thing to do . . .

'Most commendable,' said Mr. Buncombe. '*Most* commendable. That is the desire of all of us, eh, Superintendent?'

'Yes, sir,' agreed Hockley. But he wasn't committing himself any further. If he had any ideas about Mrs. Mallaby's death, he kept them to himself.

The housemaid brought in a tray of tea, staring curiously at Ann as she set it down on a low table before the fireplace. Ann removed her gloves and began to officiate at the tray as though she had lived there all her life.

Peter felt that by rights he should have taken his departure long ago, since he had more or less gate-crashed the party, but he was so interested in the girl that he was determined to stay, even at the expense of good manners. Apart from that, if he wanted to succeed in his new role of amateur detective, which he had so light-heartedly adopted, he ought to acquire as much knowledge of the case as he could.

'Sugar, Mr. Buncombe?' asked Ann, busy with the teapot.

'Thank you, one lump.' The solicitor accepted the cup she handed to him with grave courtesy.

'And you, Superintendent?'

'Please, miss,' said Hockley. 'Two lumps, if you don't mind.'

'None for me, thank you,' said Peter, anticipating the question.

'I don't like it, either,' she said. 'I think it spoils the flavour of the tea . . . Thank you.' She took a piece of anchovy toast from the plate he offered her.

'I suppose,' remarked Mr. Buncombe to Hockley as he stirred his tea, 'that you've made all the arrangements for the inquest?'

'Yes, sir,' replied the superintendent, helping himself to a piece of toast. 'It'll be held on Monday at eleven o'clock in the morning in the schoolroom. There won't be much to it. Only the evidence of identification and the medical evidence, and then we shall ask for an adjournment.'

'Very wise,' said Mr. Buncombe, nodding his head in approval. 'You are not in a position to present a case to the coroner's court at present, and the less you make public the better. The newspaper reporters will no doubt be disappointed . . .'

'Serve 'em right,' grunted Hockley with sudden feeling. 'They pestered the life out of me this morning. I had a job to get rid of 'em . . .'

'And me,' put in Peter. 'They arrived at my house before breakfast and started shooting questions at me like a machine-gun . . .'

'I hope you didn't tell 'em anything, Mr. Hunt,' broke in the superintendent.

'I don't know anything,' retorted Peter, 'so how could I?'

Ann Lexford looked at him with sudden interest.

'Mr. Hunt?' she said questioningly. 'Is

your name *Peter* Hunt?'

'It is,' replied Peter.

'Do you write books?' she went on, and when he nodded: 'Oh, I am glad to know you. I've read all your books and I liked them enormously.'

'That's very pleasant hearing,' said Peter.

'We get most of the new books at the office — for review,' she said, helping herself to cake, 'and so I am in a better position than most people. I can read all the latest books without having to pay for them.'

'That's not such pleasant hearing,' said Peter, shaking his head. 'No author likes to hear that people can get books without paying for them. There are such mundane things as royalties . . .'

'I'll make a point of buying your books in future,' said Ann, laughing. 'If you'll promise to autograph them for me.'

'That's a bargain,' answered Peter. 'I am relieved to hear that I am in no imminent danger of starvation.'

'We have a celebrated authoress among our clients,' remarked Mr. Buncombe.

'Miss — er — Drusilla Popcorn. She has, I believe, recently published her sixty-seventh novel . . . '

'She has,' said Peter without enthusiasm.

'*Passion in the Sun*,' remarked Ann with a wicked side-long glance at him. 'We have it in the office. Another cup of tea, Mr. Buncombe?'

'Thank you,' said the lawyer, passing his cup.

'The book I liked best of yours,' said Ann, pouring out tea, 'was the last one, *Summer Darkness*. The character of the girl, April, was beautifully done.'

And Peter suddenly knew why Ann Lexford had seemed so familiar to him. Of course, she was April, the heroine of his book, come to life, exactly as his imagination had pictured her. She might have stepped out of the printed pages of the book . . .

' . . . time for reading.' The voice of Hockley broke through his thoughts. 'My wife's the reader in our family. Always with a book, she is. When I do get a chance I like a good travel book . . . '

April had been one of the best pieces of creative work he had ever done, thought Peter. All the time he had been writing the book she had exercised a peculiar fascination over him. And here she was . . .

' . . . catch my train.' Mr. Buncombe, watch in hand, was speaking. 'I had better have a word with the housekeeper here before I go. I shall return on Monday for the inquest and to make arrangements for the funeral. Are you returning to London, Miss Lexford?'

'Well,' she answered, 'I did think of staying over the weekend. Is there an hotel within reasonable distance?'

'There's the 'George' at Wincaster, Miss,' said Hockley, 'or the 'Albion' . . . '

'Why not stay here?' suggested the solicitor. 'I will speak to . . . '

'Come and stay with us,' said Peter on a sudden impulse. 'My sister will be delighted . . . '

'That's very sweet of you, Mr. Hunt,' said the girl and looked as if she meant it. 'I'd like that very much, if you're sure I won't be a nuisance.'

Peter assured her, very emphatically, that she wouldn't, and it was decided that she should go back with him there and then.

Superintendent Hockley, declaring that he had a great deal of work to do, offered to give them a lift, and left with them, leaving Mr. Buncombe to settle whatever business he wished, and make his lonely way back to Wincaster by hired car, and from thence to London.

* * *

After dropping Peter and Ann Lexford at the former's gate, Superintendent Hockley drove slowly to Wincaster. The time had come, he decided, when a little quiet thinking might do a lot of good. He felt that he wanted to sort out his facts and ideas, and get them a bit more clarified.

This murder looked like being a bit of a difficult job and he didn't want to fall down on it. Unless he produced good results within a reasonable time, the Chief Constable might think of calling in Scotland Yard, and then his chance would go up like a puff of smoke.

He'd have to see that didn't happen. It wasn't likely that such a chance 'ud come his way again in a hurry. Chances didn't grow on gooseberry bushes, not round these parts . . .

Now just how far had he got?

Not so very far, when you came to look at it, but there hadn't been a lot of time, and he hadn't wasted any.

He'd established the fact that the murder must have taken place between four o'clock and half past, which was a pretty important point, and he'd found out about the cheque for five hundred pounds which looked as though it might have something to do with the motive. After the incident of that afternoon it was quite evident that Mrs. Mallaby was not all she was cracked up to be. She *had* had something to hide — that girl who had suddenly appeared out of nowhere, as you might say. Not a bit ashamed of it, either, she hadn't been. Brazen bit o' goods, in his opinion. He wondered what Emily would have thought . . .

Well, that was neither here nor there.

The thing was that there had been something in the dead woman's life that she wouldn't have wanted known. Would she have been prepared to pay somebody to keep their mouth shut? He thought she would. She'd settled down into a respectable, church-going type of woman — bit of a hypocrite from all accounts — and she certainly wouldn't have liked her past brought up and made public.

But who would have known about it?

Well, there was this Mrs. Cooper, and the girl herself — probably one or two other people as well from those early days. The snag was, that if any of these people had been blackmailing the old woman, why had they left it until now?

It seemed more likely that it was someone who had only just discovered her secret . . .

Now that was an idea. Supposing somebody local had discovered about this illegitimate daughter and threatened to make it public property unless she paid up. What about that?

She'd have paid up all right, there wasn't much doubt about that, but why should the person concerned have killed the goose that was laying the golden eggs? Surely that wasn't likely. And only one golden egg too, so far as he could see.

Perhaps Mrs. Mallaby had threatened to inform the police, and scared the blackmailer badly enough to warrant murder. That was possible.

But who was this local person who was both blackmailer and murderer? It seemed pretty obvious that it *was* a local person, or at any rate a person who knew the dead woman's habit of dropping into the church every afternoon at four o'clock . . .

There was something in what Mr. Hunt had suggested there — about alibis — though it 'ud be a bit of a job to trace everybody's whereabouts from four to half past on that particular afternoon.

It was worth considering, all the same. And he mustn't forget Billing. He'd had a pretty good opportunity, when you came to think of it.

Of course, there was always the possibility that the murder and the five hundred pounds had nothing to do with each other. Bit of a coincidence, if there wasn't a connection, but these things did happen. In that case there'd have to be some other motive . . .

What about gain?

There was money enough at stake to provide an ample motive, but who got it? Was there a will in existence that only the dead woman and the murderer knew anything about?

Hold on a minute. What was the position now that this woman, Ann Lexford, had turned up? If she was Mrs. Mallaby's daughter she'd get the estate, wouldn't she? Or would the fact that she was illegitimate make any difference?

He would have to find that out from the lawyer. He'd know.

If it didn't make any difference, well, there was the strongest motive of all. Just handed out on a plate, as you might say.

She might not have done it herself, but somebody else could have done it for her. There were quite a number of people who wouldn't stick at murder for a share of half a million quid.

The girl would, naturally, provide

herself with a good alibi, wouldn't she? She was no fool, you could see that, and she was bound to realise that she'd be the first suspect. There might be some man or other she was mixed up with — she had plenty of sex appeal, there was no gainsaying that . . .

It was well worth considering. It shouldn't be difficult to find out who her friends were, who she was intimate with, and all about 'em . . . and just where they were between four and four-thirty on that Friday afternoon . . .

Hockley sighed.

There was plenty to do, and no mistake. He looked like having all his work cut out for the next day or so and probably longer. There was plenty to follow up and that was something. It would keep the Chief Constable from getting on his hind legs and taking the matter out of his hands. So long as there were plenty of ideas to work on, he would be satisfied . . .

Tomorrow was Sunday. Well, it'ud be no day of rest for *him* that was certain. It looked like being a pretty full day so far as he could see. The wife 'ud be annoyed — not half she wouldn't. She did not like it when he had to go out on a Sunday. You couldn't blame her, really. And there was young Harry and Doris coming over for the day, too. Yes, Emily 'ud be proper riled . . .

Superintendent Hockley sighed again. Oh, well, it couldn't be helped . . .

6

The church was unusually crowded that Sunday morning and it is a regrettable fact that quite a large proportion of the congregation had come out of sheer morbid curiosity.

The empty pew, roped off, in which Mrs. Mallaby usually sat in stately reverence, and in which she had also died, was a mute reminder of the tragedy. As Miss Ginch so delicately, and so unoriginally, put it, to the speechless envy of Miss Dewsnap, who wished fervently that she had thought of it first:

'I thought that although dear, dear, Mrs. Mallaby was no longer with us in the flesh, she was hovering above us in the spirit.'

'We shall all miss her, dreadfully,' sighed Miss Dewsnap with a sniff, applying a handkerchief daintily to her thin and reddish nose.

'We shall, indeed,' said Miss Ginch.

'She was so good. Such a shining example to all of us.'

She shook her head in humble adoration of her departed friend.

'Did you see what Diana Withers had on?' asked Miss Dewsnap, lowering her voice confidentially. 'I thought it was disgusting. Showing her knees, and sitting right in the front, too.'

'Yes, indeed,' said Miss Ginch. 'The dear vicar was most shocked, I'm sure. He never took his eyes off her all through the sermon.'

'Her mother was nearly as bad,' said Miss Dewsnap severely. 'At her age, too.'

'I don't think modesty is a question of age, dear,' remarked Miss Ginch, eyeing her companion's attire critically. 'If you'll forgive me, I don't think that dress is quite suited to *you*.'

'Oh, indeed,' said Miss Dewsnap, her thin form stiffening.

'We can never see ourselves as others see us,' went on Miss Ginch spitefully, 'and perhaps a hint, now and again, dear . . . '

'It's very kind of you,' said Miss

Dewsnap in a tone that sounded as though she thought just the reverse. 'Of course, unless you are *used* to good clothes, it is very difficult to distinguish what is suitable and what is not.'

'That's exactly what I meant, dear,' said Miss Ginch with the utmost sweetness. 'I really must go now, or I shall be late getting my lunch.'

She departed in triumph, having successfully turned Miss Dewsnap's own words against her.

She hurried home and cooked her frugal lunch, and she was clearing away after the meal when there came a loud knock on the front door of her little cottage. Wondering who it could be, she opened it.

'Are you Miss Ginch?' inquired a quietly dressed man who stood on the step, and when she admitted that fact: 'I'm Superintendent Hockley, miss. I'm sorry to disturb you on a Sunday afternoon, like this, but I'm inquiring into the circumstances surrounding the death of Mrs. Mallaby and I'd like to ask you a few questions.'

'Oh dear ... yes, indeed,' said the flustered Miss Ginch and she saw, beyond the figure of the superintendent, another man just getting out of the police car. 'Please come in.'

She ushered them both, with fluttering nervousness, into the small sitting-room.

'Will you sit down? Oh, no, not that chair, if you don't mind. Uncle Frank broke the leg off and it's never been mended properly ... This is very comfortable, it was always mother's favourite.'

She darted about like a flustered hen, straightening nick-nacks and picture frames, while Hockley and Sergeant Tripp settled themselves in two extremely uncomfortable chairs and waited for her to relax. Having decided that her sitting-room was now in complete order, Miss Ginch at last sat herself down in the extreme centre of the horsehair sofa, and folded her hands in her lap. She looked at the visitors expectantly.

Hockley cleared his throat and took out his notebook.

'I believe,' he began pleasantly, 'that

you were a friend of the late Mrs. Mallaby's?'

'Oh yes,' agreed Miss Ginch with a sigh. 'It was a great blow to me when I heard the dreadful news.'

'Quite so. I'm sure it must have been,' murmured the superintendent, sympathetically. 'Did Mrs. Mallaby every say, or do, anything that suggested that she was in fear of somebody?'

'Good gracious,' exclaimed the startled Miss Ginch. 'No, indeed. Why should she be in fear of somebody?'

'You didn't notice any change in her manner recently?' continued Hockley. 'As though she might have been worried, or troubled, about anything?'

Miss Ginch shook her head.

'No, I never noticed anything like that at all,' she declared.

'Do you think that if she had had anything on her mind, she would have mentioned it to you?'

Miss Ginch considered this with her head on one side, like a bird that has been disturbed by some strange sound.

'I really don't think I can truthfully

say,' she answered after a pause. 'Dear Mrs. Mallaby had a very strong will. If she had anything troubling her, I think she would have kept it to herself.'

'I see,' said Hockley. 'Did she ever make you a confidant in any of her affairs?'

'Oh yes,' said Miss Ginch with pride. 'In quite a number of matters connected with the parish, you know. She was very outspoken about anything that she considered wrong. I admired her courage so much in that respect . . .'

'It made her very unpopular, I suppose?' suggested Hockley.

Miss Ginch tossed her head.

'With some people,' she answered. 'Those who failed to appreciate the purity of her motives and her high sense of duty. When we try to live up to a high Christian standard we are sometimes greatly misunderstood.' She conveyed that this had been her own unhappy experience.

'In your opinion, Mrs. Mallaby lived up to this standard?'

'Oh yes!' declared Miss Ginch, raising

her eyes to the ceiling and clasping her hands ecstatically. 'Oh yes.'

'With the result that she made a good many enemies?'

'I fear so.'

'Are you aware of anyone in particular?'

'Well, no . . . I don't think I am.'

'Can you suggest anyone who bore a grudge or hated her enough to wish to bring about her death?'

'No, no, I can't imagine anyone being so wicked.'

Superintendent Hockley glanced at the open page of his notebook.

'On the Monday before she was murdered,' he said, 'she drew five hundred pounds from the United Capital Bank in one-pound notes. Have you any idea for what reason she drew this large sum of money?'

Miss Ginch looked startled. Her small eyes narrowed and her thin lips parted.

'Good gracious me!' she exclaimed. 'What could she have wanted all that money for?'

'That's what I'm asking you, miss,' said the superintendent.

'I've really no idea,' said Miss Ginch. 'I know nothing whatever about it. Perhaps that is why she was killed . . . '

'What do you mean?' asked Hockley quickly.

'Well, if someone knew that she had all this money in her possession,' said Miss Ginch, 'might they not have killed her in order to obtain it?'

This was a point that had not occurred to Hockley and he considered it for a moment in silence.

'Was she in the habit of carrying large sums of money about with her?' he asked.

'No,' answered Miss Ginch. 'Only a very few shillings as a rule. She paid everything by cheque, you see.'

'Then it seems very strange that she should have carried a large sum like five hundred pounds about with her,' said the superintendent. 'In one-pound notes it would have been pretty bulky . . . '

Miss Ginch wrinkled her narrow forehead.

'I can't think why she should have wanted all that money,' she said.

'I understand that she was very

generous with regard to the church,' said Hockley. 'Could she have . . . '

'Oh no,' broke in Miss Ginch. 'She would have told *me* if she had made a donation to the church funds. She *always* told everybody.'

'Maybe it was some charity she was interested in?' suggested the superintendent.

'She never gave anything to charities,' declared Miss Ginch emphatically. 'She didn't approve of charities at all.'

Hockley tried several other questions in the same vein, but only drew a blank. Miss Ginch, very obviously, knew nothing of the destination of the five hundred pounds. He switched to a different subject.

'Did you know,' he said slowly and deliberately, 'that Mrs. Mallaby had a daughter?'

Miss Ginch was so taken aback by this question that her false teeth, never very firmly fixed, almost fell out of her mouth. She managed to prevent them falling completely, however, and stared at the superintendent in consternation.

'A daughter?' she repeated. 'Good gracious me! Surely you must be mistaken? Poor dear Mrs. Mallaby's marriage was childless . . . '

'I am aware of that,' said Hockley. 'The child I am speaking about was born several years before her marriage.'

'Several years before . . . ' breathed Miss Ginch, her eyes alight with interest and excitement. 'Do you mean . . . she was married twice?'

'No,' said the superintendent briefly.

The full significance of this statement took some time to permeate Miss Ginch's brain. When it did, and the full horror of the allegation became clear, she gasped as though she had suddenly been dipped in icy water.

'Oh,' she said, 'you don't mean . . . you can't . . . It cannot possibly be true . . . '

'There's no doubt about it, miss,' said Hockley. 'I've met the young lady, myself.'

In such prosaic manner he turned the idol's feet to clay. Miss Ginch gobbled spasmodically — that was the only word for it — before she could speak plainly.

'I can't believe it,' she whispered faintly. 'It's too, too dreadful . . . Oh, that she could have been so wicked and deceitful, a whited sepulchre . . . '

What would Miss Dewsnap say when she knew? And the dear vicar? What would everybody say? Miss Ginch gave a little shiver of excitement in anticipation of the tit-bit which her eager tongue was itching to spread abroad. Mrs. Mallaby's duplicity would lack nothing in the telling. The unsuspected clay feet of the idol would receive a full exposure at her hands. Miss Ginch's righteous indignation was thoroughly aroused.

Superintendent Hockley's shrewd eyes saw the various expressions that came and went on her face and guessed, pretty accurately, what was taking place in the turmoil of her mind.

'You knew nothing about this daughter?' he asked.

'I?' Miss Ginch's voice was shrill with indignation. 'No, indeed. I would never have given my friendship to her if I'd known the sort of woman she really was. She deceived me, grossly and flagrantly.'

'Quite so,' Hockley cut short the threatened tirade. 'Now, miss, when was the last time you saw Mrs. Mallaby?'

Miss Ginch frowned in an effort of concentration.

'Let me see,' she said. 'Was it on Tuesday? No, it must have been the Wednesday . . . Yes, I'm sure it was . . . the Wednesday morning. Yes, it was. I met her in the High Street, shopping.'

'You're quite sure that was the last time?' persisted Hockley. 'You didn't see her on the Friday — the day she was murdered?'

Miss Ginch was convinced she had not seen her on the Friday.

'Would you mind telling us, miss,' said the superintendent casually, 'where you were on the Friday afternoon, say from three until five?'

She informed him, after a moment's thought, that she had been lying down in her bedroom. She had had a very bad headache — she suffered from bad headaches. Immediately after lunch she had taken two aspirins, and spent the rest of the afternoon lying on her bed in a darkened room. She had fallen asleep and had not wakened until a quarter past five, by which time her headache had gone. No, there was nobody who could substantiate this statement. How could there be? She did not employ a maid. Her income was too small for such luxuries.

Hockley made a note of her reply and got up.

'Well, I think that's all for now, miss,' he said, 'I'm very much obliged to you.'

As soon as he had left with the silent Sergeant Tripp, Miss Ginch hurried up the stairs, put on her hat, and tripped lightly out to call on her dear friend Miss Dewsnap. Her mouth was literally watering in anticipation of the effect the news that she had learned that afternoon would have on that angular and sometimes irritating lady.

★   ★   ★

Margaret Hunt had taken to Ann Lexford at once, and Peter was glad to see that the liking was mutual.

'I suppose,' he remarked as they were

having coffee in the drawing-room after lunch, 'that you'll be coming to the inquest tomorrow?'

Ann nodded.

'You'll cause a sensation,' remarked Margaret. 'The whole of the village will turn out to get a glimpse of you.'

Ann laughed.

'I hope they won't be disappointed,' she said. 'Poor mother. How she would have hated it.'

Peter privately agreed with her. Mrs. Mallaby, dragged from her throne of righteous eminence, would have suffered untold degradation. He had no illusions as to how her so-called friends would react when they heard the news. It was better for her that somebody had ended her life — better and more merciful.

'Hockley hasn't let the grass grow under his feet,' he said. 'He seems to be a pretty sound chap.'

'You'll have to get a move on, if you intend to steal his thunder,' remarked his sister.

'Why, what's he going to do?' asked Ann. She put down her empty coffee cup and looked inquiringly from one to the other.

'What isn't he going to do?' said Margaret with a grimace. 'He's going to play the Great Detective, that's what he's going to do. At least he's going to try. He's decided to solve the mystery off his own bat.'

'Oh, are you, Peter?' exclaimed Ann with sudden interest.

'Well . . . ' began Peter hesitantly.

'That's what you said yesterday,' broke in Margaret. 'So don't try and squirm out of it. You said . . . '

'I know what I said, and I meant it,' interrupted Peter. 'I think it would be interesting to try, anyway.'

'So do I,' said Ann, excitedly. 'I wish I could help . . . '

'Why don't you?' suggested Peter eagerly. 'Between us we ought to be a match for Hockley.'

Ann shook her head.

'I've got to go back to London tomorrow,' she said regretfully. 'Otherwise . . . '

'Must you go back?' asked Peter.

'Couldn't you stay a bit longer?'

'It sounds very tempting,' said Ann thoughtfully. 'I suppose I could take a week off . . . I don't want to be a nuisance though . . . '

'You needn't worry about *that*,' put in Margaret quickly. 'You're welcome to stay as long as you like — the longer the better, so far as I'm concerned.'

'And me,' said Peter promptly. 'What about it Ann?'

'You both sound as if you really meant it,' said Ann laughing. 'I think it's very sweet of you. I'll ring up first thing in the morning and, if I can get the time off, I'll stop. I've often thought I'd make a good Doctor Watson.'

'You'll probably end by being Sherlock Holmes as well,' said Margaret. 'Why Peter should imagine that he's cut out for the role of the Great Detective, I haven't the faintest idea. He can never find *anything* as a rule . . . '

'That,' said Peter, 'is a monstrous slander. I can always find things if they're left where I put 'em. But after you've had an orgy of tidiness, I defy even Sherlock

Holmes to find anything.'

'Perhaps the murderer has had an orgy of tidiness, as you call it, and tidied himself away,' retorted Margaret, trying to coax a flame out of a small and obstinate lighter.

'We shall explore every avenue and leave no stone unturned,' said Peter solemnly. 'That is the correct thing to say when you haven't the faintest idea what to do next.' He took a box of matches from his pocket and gave her a light.

'Thanks,' said Margaret, eyeing the matchbox with interest. 'Where did you get that box of matches, by the way?'

'I bought it,' returned Peter airily. 'How do you suppose I got it?'

'From the kitchen,' answered his sister promptly. 'That's where you usually get your matches. I can't keep a box anywhere in the house for longer than five minutes,' she explained, turning to Ann. 'They all find their way, in some mysterious fashion, into Peter's pocket. He always swears that he's never touched them, so I suppose they fly there of their own accord.'

'You shouldn't leave them about,' said Ann, laughing. 'From what my friends tell me, men and matches seem to have a fatal attraction for each other.'

'I'm afraid,' said Peter, 'that you are getting quite the wrong impression of my domestic habits.'

'I don't think so,' said Ann. 'I'm quite prepared to believe Margaret.'

She uncrossed her legs and leaned back in her chair, smiling at him.

'I was afraid of that,' he said and sighed. 'Oh well, a prophet is always without honour in his own country.'

'That depends a great deal upon the prophet,' said Margaret. 'When are you going to start being a detective?'

'After the inquest,' replied Peter, settling himself comfortably on the settee, and hitching a cushion under his head.

'You're wasting a marvellous opportunity,' said Margaret, shaking her head. 'By all the canons of tradition you ought to leap up, just before the verdict, and cry in a ringing voice: 'There is your man, Inspector', and point to the Coroner, or someone equally unlikely. I do wish you would do that, Peter. It would be such fun.'

'I wish you'd take this more seriously,' said Peter. 'After all, murder has been done — a real murder, and not a very pleasant one at that. And it affects Ann pretty closely.'

'Oh, I'm sorry.' The mischief died out of Margaret's eyes, and she turned a suddenly grave and contrite face to Ann. 'I never thought . . . '

'Don't worry about me,' said Ann quickly. 'I can't pretend to have any deep feeling over it. She was as much a stranger to me as — as anyone. If I pretended to feel even grieved about it, I should only be a hypocrite . . . '

'All the same, Peter's quite right,' said Margaret seriously. 'She was murdered and I shouldn't joke about it.' She threw the remains of her cigarette into the fire and stretched out her long legs. 'I don't see how you propose to make a start,' she continued, clasping her hands behind her head. 'So far, it looks as though you have the entire population of the village to choose from.'

'It's not quite as bad as that,' said Peter. 'There must be a motive. That's what we've got to look for.'

'But how?' asked Ann. 'You can't just go to people and say: 'Look here, did you have any reason for killing Mrs. Mallaby?''

'They'd all say 'yes',' interposed Margaret, 'if they spoke the truth.'

'I suppose we look for the most obvious motive first,' said Peter thoughtfully. 'I believe most murders are committed for gain. Mrs. Mallaby was an exceedingly rich woman, so the first thing to ask is, who stands to gain by her death.'

'Well, I suppose if she died without making a will, I do,' said Ann quietly.

Peter looked at her in sudden and startled comprehension. Of course. Why hadn't he thought of that before blundering into speech? If she could prove that she was the late Mrs. Mallaby's daughter, she would be the next of kin. It wouldn't make any difference, legally, that she was illegitimate . . .

'I should think it was very unlikely that she didn't make a will,' continued Ann.

'Anyway, you can leave me out as a possible suspect. I wouldn't touch a penny of her money under any consideration.'

'I should never have suspected you, anyway,' said Peter truthfully. 'It never crossed my mind . . . '

'Well, then, it should,' retorted Ann. 'If you're going to be any use as a detective, you mustn't let personal prejudices come into it.'

'It's ridiculous to suspect Doctor Watson,' retorted Peter. 'That's outside all the rules of the game. It just isn't done. Besides you've got an alibi. You were in your office in London all Friday afternoon. The person we want must have been in Long Manton. The murder was committed between four o'clock and half past. Anyone with an alibi for that time is automatically ruled out.'

'Well, then it's easy,' commented Margaret lazily. 'All you've got to do is to ask everybody where they were on Friday afternoon at that time. If they can't tell you, put 'em down on your list of suspects right away.'

Peter grinned.

'Right,' he said, 'we'll start with you. Where were you between four o'clock and four-thirty on Friday afternoon?'

'Me?' exclaimed his sister. 'Why I was . . . wait a moment, where *was* I?'

'I'm waiting for you to tell us,' said Peter sternly.

'You know very well where I was,' said Margaret suddenly. 'I was lying on that settee, reading a book. You got up against a snag in your work and decided to go for a walk . . . '

'That was at a quarter to four,' interrupted Peter. 'I left the house at a quarter to four. What did you do?'

'I stayed where I was until nearly five and then I got up and made tea,' answered his sister promptly. 'I was expecting you back . . . '

'Who's going to substantiate that?' asked Peter, blandly.

Margaret looked at him in surprise.

'Well, there was nobody here but me . . . '

'Exactly,' broke in Peter triumphantly. 'So you haven't got an alibi that 'ud hold water. And that's what you'd find in six cases out of ten. By the time you'd gone through the whole village you'd have a list of suspects large enough to fill a good-sized notebook.'

'But surely quite a number of them could be eliminated,' said Ann. 'People don't commit murder for the sake of it. There'd be a reason . . . '

'There might not even be that,' he answered seriously. 'Not what we'd call a reason. The people round here are a queer lot. Quite a few of them are mentally unbalanced. They're not insane, but they're on the borderline. Psychopathic cases. Suppressed emotions, inhibitions and all the rest of it. When you get a bunch of people like that something's got to go, sooner or later, and when it does, it's usually pretty unpleasant.'

'But do you seriously suggest that someone would commit a murder just for the sake of it?' asked Ann doubtfully.

'It's possible,' answered Peter.

'You're arguing against yourself now,' said Margaret. 'Just now you said the first thing to look for was a motive. Make up your mind.'

'I still say that's the first thing to look for,' replied her brother. 'But you've got to take everything into consideration.'

'Well, I should exhaust every other possibility before you start to look for a homicidal lunatic,' said Margaret.

'I shall,' answered Peter. 'And do you know the first person I'm going to be very interested in?'

'Who?' demanded Margaret.

'Billing,' answered Peter.

7

It was very late that Sunday night when Superintendent Hockley reached his home. He was very tired and, in consequence, slightly dispirited.

Young Harry and his wife had long since taken their departure in order to catch the last bus, and Mrs. Hockley, yawning, and still a little disgruntled over the absence of her husband on the one day when she considered she had a right to expect him to be home, was contemplating going to bed, and had already undressed and arrayed herself in an old padded blue dressing-gown with that end in view.

The superintendent's supper was laid ready for him on the kitchen table: cold mutton, pickles, cheese, and a bottle of Guinness.

While he ate slowly, munching each mouthful with great deliberation, for he suffered from incipient indigestion, his wife recounted such items of information as she had acquired during the day which she thought would interest him.

His mother had had trouble with the lodger and had given him notice; Maureen's baby had cut its first tooth; young Harry had done so well in his new job that his employer had given him a rise; Doris had got a new coat which didn't suit her a bit, and the tap in the sink wanted a new washer, etc., etc.

Hockley listened with half his tired brain, using the other half to go over the day's work, with the result that he was not always quite certain what she had said, and replied to most of her remarks with a noncommittal grunt that could have meant anything. He was greatly relieved when Mrs. Hockley took herself off to bed with a final injunction 'not to be long.'

He finished his meal, drew up a chair to the dying fire in the kitchen range, and filled and lit his pipe. While he smoked he went over in his mind the result of the day's work and found the contemplation not very edifying.

In company with Sergeant Tripp he had conducted a series of interviews with some of the inhabitants of Long Manton and the result had not been very profitable.

At Colonel Bramber's they had drawn a complete blank. The Colonel had been indoors during the whole of Friday afternoon with Mrs. Bramber, who had had a relapse and was completely prostrate. They could offer no information that was likely to be of any help. They both, obviously, resented the disturbance of their Sunday peace.

Miss Dewsnap had been in the post office until six o'clock. She could not bring anyone to prove that she was there during the vital period of four to four-thirty, no customers had come in during that time, but she could hardly have left the shop to look after itself, so Hockley was inclined to believe her. She stated that there were quite a number of people who had disliked Mrs. Mallaby, but she refused to be more explicit than that. She could offer no helpful suggestions at all.

The landlord of the Fox and Hounds, Mr. Penny, was equally unhelpful. He had been out on the Friday afternoon in question, until just after five, but he had not been in the neighbourhood of the church, or anywhere near it. He usually took a walk in the afternoon as far out in the open country as he could and that afternoon he had walked to Ashley Woods, about four miles away. He thought the village would be a better place without Mrs. Mallaby, and quite a lot of other people too, if you asked him. He couldn't help in any way. He knew nothing. He attended to his business which was to sell beer, and didn't concern himself with other people's business. It would be a good thing if other people did the same.

Mr. Boggs was also desirous of having nothing to do with it. He hadn't liked Mrs. Mallaby and he considered that 'she had got what she asked for' but he had had no personal grudge against her except 'that she had been a difficult customer to please.' He had been busy getting a consignment ready for sale on the Saturday and hadn't left his shop until after six.

Mr. Withers had been working in the bank until five-fifteen and had then gone straight home. His wife and his daughter had both spent the afternoon at home, according to them, but there was nobody to substantiate this. Mr. and Mrs. Conway had been out for a walk together. They had been out from three o'clock until four forty-five. They had met nobody they knew. Again there was only their word for it.

There was only one thing that seemed certain. That was the almost general dislike of the dead woman. Those people who hadn't openly admitted that they had disliked her, showed the fact by the way they spoke of her.

But dislike wasn't a very good motive for murder.

Well, the day's work hadn't got him very far, he thought ruefully. Still it was early days yet. He'd have to have something for the Chief Constable soon, but no man could do miracles, and it was a difficult business, no matter which way you looked at it . . .

What could the dead woman have wanted the five hundred pounds for? And what had happened to it? There was something in what Miss Ginch had said, that the murderer had pinched it. But would Mrs. Mallaby have carried it about with her all that time? It was hardly likely. No, she'd drawn it out for some special purpose, to pay somebody for some reason or other. There he was, back again at blackmail. That could only be the reason why she had drawn that money out in one-pound notes. And there was a reason for blackmail. That daughter . . . It wouldn't hurt to know something more about her. Not that he really believed that she had anything to do with it . . . There was the inquest in the morning . . .

Superintendent Hockley found himself nodding. He got up, gave himself a little shake, put out the light, carefully locked the front door and went to bed, where Mrs. Hockley was already in the throes of a noisy slumber.

★ ★ ★

Monday morning was dark and gloomy, with masses of low cloud driven before a north wind. It was cold too. Not a sharp invigorating cold, but a damp, stealthy cold that insinuated itself beneath the warmest clothing and chilled the marrow.

Ann telephoned to her office at ten o'clock and, to Peter's undisguised delight, was able to arrange for a week's holiday.

Quite apart from her extraordinary resemblance to the girl he had created in his book, a resemblance that grew more marked the better he came to know her, she attracted and interested him as no other woman had ever done before. It was not only her attractiveness in looks, there was something else, a certain quality of mind that he found unusually stimulating.

She could talk, and she could talk well. She had ideas that were not just a re-hash of the newspapers or something she had read in books, but original and sometimes startling. You felt when you talked to her, that she had not only taken the trouble to think — a rare thing in these enlightened days — but had thought about something that was really worth thinking about.

Quite a lot of her ideas, Peter agreed with, but there were some he did not. She had, however, the rare ability to argue without losing her temper, and also to see another person's point of view.

Margaret took an instant liking to her. She had the gift of making you feel like an old friend even though you had only known her for a short while, and was completely unselfconscious or affected.

Peter was glad that she was going to stay longer. How Mrs. Mallaby had ever succeeded in producing such a daughter was a mystery. He could only conclude that Ann had taken after her unknown father.

When they reached the schoolroom for the inquest there was already a large crowd gathered outside, although it was only a quarter to eleven. Peter recognised a number of reporters, and one in particular whom he knew rather well — a man called Gould, who was on the *Morning Sun*, and who had not put in an appearance before.

He was a small, thin man, in a shabby raincoat, and he was puffing at a pipe, near the entrance to the school-house.

Colonel Bramber, with Mrs. Bramber clinging to his arm, stood on the fringe of the crowd. That chronic invalid had apparently undergone a miraculous cure in ample time to satisfy her curiosity concerning the proceedings. Miss Ginch was there, too, talking volubly to Miss Dewsnap, and so were Mr. and Mrs. Conway.

In fact, nearly the entire population of Long Manton had turned out for the free entertainment.

'They'll never get them all in the schoolroom,' said Peter. 'I foresee much wailing and gnashing of teeth.'

Mr. Buncombe arrived in the hired car, dignified, pompous, and immaculately dressed. He was eyed with interest as he bowed to Ann and Margaret, and wished Peter a stately 'good morning.'

The harassed constable who was guarding the door, received an instruction from some hidden individual inside, and began to admit the crowd.

They pressed forward in a solid wedge, and the doorway quickly became jammed. The constable, somehow or other, managed to sort them all out, and just before eleven struck from the tower of St. Mary's, all those who could be squeezed in were inside and the door closed in the faces of the unlucky ones.

There was a great deal of whispering and nudging as Ann took her place beside Peter and the solicitor. Miss Ginch had done her work well, and the fact that Mrs. Mallaby had had an illegitimate daughter was known to everyone in Long Manton. Stares of disapproval were directed towards Ann, and she was obviously being discussed avidly, if inaudibly.

Although she was perfectly aware of this, it did not embarrass her in the least.

'I seem to have caused a flutter in the hen-coop,' she remarked calmly to Peter. He made a grimace at her and grinned, and at that moment the Coroner arrived.

The jury was sworn in, and the Coroner made a short opening speech, explaining why they were there, after which Mr. Buncombe was taken to view the body.

He testified that it was that of his client, Mrs. Mallaby, and that he had last seen her at the beginning of April, when he had come to Manton Lodge to transact certain business that had nothing to do with the inquiry.

Mr. Billing, the verger, was next called, and he gave evidence concerning the discovery of the body, making the most of his short appearance in the limelight.

Peter explained how he had been passing the church when Mr. Billing had called to him, and what had subsequently happened.

Police-constable Rutt, looking very important, next took the stand. He told the jury how he had been called by Billing to the church, and in great detail, exactly what steps he had taken when he had seen what had happened.

The Coroner gave him a word of commendation, which was what he obviously expected, and his place was taken by Doctor Pratt.

He gave the cause and probable time of death, described the wound, and gave it as his opinion that it could not possibly have been self-inflicted.

Asked about the probable weapon used, he said that it was a thin, short-bladed, very sharp instrument, and might have been a penknife, or similar object.

The police surgeon came next and confirmed everything that Doctor Pratt had said.

There was an anticipatory murmur when Superintendent Hockley was called, but if the people expected anything sensational, they were disappointed.

In a stolid, unemotional voice, Hockley described his arrival on the scene of the crime and the investigations he had made. It was all very matter-of-fact and business-like.

When he had finished, the Coroner, as though he had received his cue, said:

'I understand the police would like an adjournment in order to collect further evidence?'

'That's right, sir,' said Hockley.

'Very well. I shall adjourn this inquiry for a fortnight,' said the Coroner, to the disappointment of his audience and the reporters, who had hoped for something sensational.

The crowd began the scramble for the door, and Peter, seeing Mr. Gould standing a little uncertainly by himself, went over and spoke to him.

'Hello, Gould, how are you?' he said. 'Nothing very exciting for you this morning, is there?'

The reporter looked at him with watery eyes. He always appeared as though he had a cold in his head.

'How d'you do, Mr. Hunt,' he said in a husky voice. 'No, nothing very exciting, as you say. Who is that lady over there?' He nodded towards the door through which Mr. and Mrs. Conway were making their way in the wake of several other people.

'Which one?' asked Peter. 'Do you mean the one with the man in the camel-hair coat?'

Gould nodded.

'That's the one,' he said.

'That's Mrs. Conway,' said Peter.

'Oh, is that what she calls herself now,' murmured the reporter.

Peter stared at him.

'Calls herself *now*,' he repeated. 'What do you mean?'

'The last time I saw her,' said Gould deliberately, 'she was in the dock at the Old Bailey on a charge of poisoning her husband. Her name was Mrs. Lucas then. She was acquitted . . . '

'You must have made a mistake . . . ' began Peter, but the reporter shook his head.

'It was eleven years ago,' he said, 'but I've got a good memory, Mr. Hunt. I haven't made any mistake. That's Mrs. Lucas.'

★ ★ ★

Peter Hunt, Superintendent Hockley and Gould sat in the living-room at Peter's house, whence Hockley had driven them, at Peter's suggestion, after the inquest.

Margaret had made them a large pot of coffee, set it on a table before them, and diplomatically vanished into the dining-room with Ann, leaving them to their own devices.

'This is very interesting what you tell

146

me, Mr. Gould,' remarked the superintendent, setting down his cup after a huge gulp of steaming coffee. 'I remember the Lucas case; quite a stir it made at the time. I read all the reports in the newspapers. You're quite sure that this Mrs. Conway is the same woman?'

'Quite,' affirmed the reporter. 'I can't afford to make mistakes in my job, any more than you can in yours.'

'We all do, now and again, whether we can afford it or not,' said Hockley with a wry smile.

'There's no mistake about this,' declared Gould emphatically. 'She's the same woman right enough. She looks a little older, but she hasn't changed all that much.'

'If I recollect rightly,' said Hockley, screwing up his face in an effort of memory, 'Lucas died from an overdose of sleeping pills. Veronal. Traces of veronal were found in a glass of hot milk which Mrs. Lucas had given him the last thing at night, because he had a cold. It was also proved that she had bought a bottle of the pills the day before.'

'That's right,' said Gould, nodding. 'She admitted that. She said she had been sleeping badly and that her doctor had given her a prescription. The doctor confirmed her statement. She had a hell of a life with Lucas, who appeared to be an unpleasant devil in every way. There were other women and he drank. The defence put forward a strong plea that he was mentally unbalanced, and bolstered it up with the fact that he had spent two years in a mental home in his youth. It was quite possible, they affirmed, that he had taken the veronal himself during a fit of depression, and for lack of sufficient evidence, the jury acquitted Mrs. Lucas. The general opinion was that she was very lucky.'

'You mean, you think she did it?' asked Peter.

'I don't think there's any doubt about it,' declared Gould. 'Most people thought so, too, at the time. She disappeared completely after the trial . . . '

'And now she's turned up again,' remarked Hockley thoughtfully. 'She must have married Conway in the interval.' He drank the remainder of his coffee. 'The question is, has she got anything to do with this business?'

'I can't see why she should,' said Peter, who liked little Mrs. Conway. 'After all, this happened eleven years ago and had nothing whatever to do with Mrs. Mallaby . . . '

'Well, Mr. Hunt,' interrupted the superintendent, 'I don't see how we can be sure of that. Supposing Mrs. Mallaby had found out about her past? She'd know what a scandalmonger she was and that the whole story, which she'd succeeded in living down, was likely to blaze up again. She'd had a taste of respectability an' happiness, and she'd try to hang on to it at any cost. There's a pretty big motive for murder there, sir.'

'And having got away with one, she'd be all the more likely to try again,' put in Gould. 'They always do. But they seldom change the method. A poisoner will invariably use poison . . . '

'If it's practicable,' said Hockley, 'and there's an opportunity. Maybe in this case it wasn't practicable and there wasn't an opportunity. She'd have to act quickly, before Mrs. Mallaby got a chance to spread the news around.'

'How would she have known that Mrs. Mallaby had found out about her?' demanded Peter. 'It's unlikely she would have told Mrs. Conway and nobody else.'

'Well, I don't know about that, sir,' said Hockley, shaking his head. 'Mrs. Conway disliked Mrs. Mallaby very much indeed. From what I can make out, she was always saying what an unpleasant woman she was, an' I expect Mrs. Mallaby knew about it. What's more likely than that she should meet Mrs. Conway, after she'd found out about her, and say something like this: 'I know all about you and what happened eleven years ago, and before long everybody else'll know about it too.' It's just the sort of thing she would do, from all accounts. She'd know that it 'ud make Mrs. Conway squirm and, being the type of woman she was, she'd have liked that.'

Peter was forced to admit that Mrs. Mallaby would, most certainly, have liked that.

'You've got to show that she had an opportunity,' he said. 'She may be able to produce an alibi for the time the murder must have been committed . . . '

'That's just what she can't do, sir,' said Hockley quietly. 'Leastways, not a sound one. She was out for a walk with her husband.'

'Which means that he must be in it, too, if she did the murder,' said Peter, and Hockley nodded.

'There'd be nothing very unlikely in that, sir, if he was fond of his wife,' remarked the superintendent.

'You think they planned it together?' said Peter doubtfully.

'Not necessarily, sir,' said Hockley. 'He may not have known anything about it until she'd done it. Then, naturally, he'd try an' give her an alibi.'

'H'm,' grunted Peter. 'It's all conjecture, isn't it? There isn't an atom of proof.'

'No, sir, but it gives us something to work on,' said Hockley, thinking of the report to the Chief Constable.

'For heaven's sake make certain that there hasn't been a mistake,' said Peter, 'before you work on anything. Gould may be wrong. There's such a thing as a 'double.' He may have been led away by a resemblance . . . '

'You needn't run away with that idea,' broke in the reporter. 'There's no doubt at all. Mrs. Lucas had a small mole at the side of her nose. So has Mrs. Conway. No 'double' would get as close at that.'

'Well, even if you are right,' said Peter, 'she may have had nothing to do with this affair. For the Lord's sake don't go and rake up all the unpleasantness, which she thinks is over, until you're quite sure. It would be horribly unfair.'

'You needn't worry, sir,' said Hockley, reassuringly. 'I'm not going to make a song and dance about this, I promise you. And I rely on Mr. Gould not to print anything . . . '

'Oh, I say, look here,' expostulated the reporter, 'this is a good story . . . '

'Maybe it is,' said Hockley firmly. 'But I don't want it in the newspapers. If you print a word there'll be trouble, so I'm warning you. Perhaps it'll develop into a better story later on, then you can go ahead — when I say the word.'

Gould was disgruntled. The 'scoop' he had planned had been nipped even before it had a chance to bud. But Hockley was adamant, and no amount of arguing and pleading would shift him. He would have no premature publicity spoiling his investigation, and Peter was in full agreement with him.

Gould and Hockley left together shortly after, and Peter went in search of Ann and Margaret.

He found them in the dining-room, and told them what had happened.

'Mary Conway's a nice little woman,' declared Margaret. 'I don't believe she had anything to do with it.'

'Nice little women have killed people before,' said Peter. 'And in spite of the fact that she was acquitted, it seems to be the general belief that she poisoned her first husband.'

'The worst about anybody is always generally believed,' retorted Margaret. 'She was acquitted, and according to the laws of the land, she's innocent. It's a scandalous shame to hold it against her.'

'I think so, too,' agreed Ann. 'Because, by sheer coincidence, she should have chosen to make a new life for herself in a place where another murder happens, it's ridiculous to jump to the conclusion that she did it.'

'Nobody's jumping to conclusions,' said Peter. 'Not even Hockley. He's only considering it as a possibility, and you've got to admit that it is.'

'I don't believe for a moment she did it,' said Margaret, obstinately.

'What do you think, Peter?' asked Ann. 'Do you think she did it?'

'I've a completely open mind,' declared Peter. 'Somebody did it, and that's all I'm prepared to say.'

'Brilliant deduction by the Great Detective,' cried Margaret sarcastically. 'What you need, Peter, are two violins and a bucket of cocaine, and to try and become intelligent.'

★ ★ ★

'Well, that's over,' said Mary Conway, taking off her coat and hat, and patting her hair into place in front of the mirror over the fireplace. 'Not very exciting, was it?'

'What did you expect?' asked her husband humorously. 'The dramatic arrest of the murderer?'

'No,' answered his wife, stirring the fire into a blaze, 'but I thought we should have heard more. That girl who was with Peter Hunt and his sister is the daughter, I suppose?'

'Yes. She looked rather nice,' said her husband.

'Very attractive,' agreed Mrs. Conway. 'Did you see the black looks she was getting from the Ginch lot? I bet they had a shock when they found that their dear Mrs. Mallaby had an illegitimate child. I can't imagine how the woman ever contrived to be so human.'

'*De mortuis,*' murmured Conway.

'That's all rubbish,' said his wife. 'Because a person's dead it doesn't alter them — what they were, I mean. Why whitewash them?'

'Why not just forget all about 'em?' he suggested with a smile. 'If you can't say anything nice about them, why say anything at all?'

She came over to him, bent down quickly, and kissed the top of his head.

'You're a nice man,' she said affectionately. 'The longer I know you the nicer I think you are.'

He caught her hand, caressing the fingers gently.

'You're a nice woman, Mary,' he said.

'Quite a lot of people don't think so,' she answered.

'They don't know you, not like I do,' he said. 'If they did, they couldn't think anything wrong of you.'

'Maybe you are more right than they are,' she whispered. She lingered a moment or two by his chair, her hand in his. Then she gently freed herself.

'I must get the lunch on,' she said briskly, and hurried into the kitchen.

Conway sat on, staring into the fire. He remembered his first meeting with this woman who was now his wife. In an obscure little Cornish fishing village, it had been, whither he had gone for a holiday. She had been a timid, scared girl with sad eyes, nervous and constantly wary, as though she expected in some vague way to be hurt. He had seen the same expression once on the face of an ill-treated child.

In that queer way, for which there is no practical explanation, they were instantly and mutually attracted to each other. On his side it began with an overwhelming sympathy and a desire to mitigate in some way her obvious loneliness. On hers an immediate response to kindness and friendly companionship. They each found something in the other that seemed to fulfil a long-felt want and made them both complete . . .

Three weeks after he had first met her, Conway proposed and she refused him. It was then he heard her story, told with a directness and candour that was harsh — almost brutal . . .

They were married a month later and he had never been happier in his life. Gradually he had seen his wife lose that scared, hurt expression, and laughter come back to her lips and eyes.

They had found the house on the Green in Long Manton and settled down, hoping to find peace and happiness, and, for Mary, forgetfulness of that period in her life to which neither of them ever referred. They found all three . . .

'You're very quiet,' called Mary from the kitchen. 'What are you doing?'

'Just thinking,' he answered.

'Well, if you've nothing better to do,' she called, laughing, 'you can come and peel the potatoes.'

He went through into the kitchen and found her with her sleeves rolled up above the elbow, her hands immersed in a bowl of flour.

'What are you making?' he asked.

'Apple pudding,' she answered. 'If you'll do the potatoes it'll be a help. They're over in the sink.'

The potatoes were peeled and ready, and the pudding boiling merrily, when the knock came at the door.

'Who can that be?' said Mrs. Conway, frowning. 'See who it is, dear. My hands are all wet . . . '

He went to the front door and opened

it. On the step stood Superintendent Hockley.

'I'm sorry to trouble you,' he said apologetically, 'but I should like a word with your wife.'

'What is it this time?' demanded Conway, a little irritably. 'We've told you all we know . . . '

'I just want to confirm an item of information that has reached me,' answered Hockley. 'It won't take very long.'

'Who is it?' called Mrs. Conway, and she appeared in the tiny hall, wiping her hands on her apron.

'The police want to ask some more questions, dear,' grunted her husband. 'I suppose you'd better come in,' he added rather ungraciously to Hockley.

The superintendent came in and was conducted to the sitting-room.

'Lunch is nearly ready,' said Mrs. Conway. 'I hope . . . '

'What I have to say, ma'am, won't take more than a few minutes,' said Hockley. 'I'm given to understand that before your marriage to Mr. Conway you were a Mrs.

Lucas. Is that right?'

He saw, almost before the words had left his lips, that it *was* right. The colour faded from her face so that the rouge on each cheek stood out, nakedly and crudely, for what it was. She was standing near a chair and her hands groped for, and found, the back of it and clutched it convulsively. She stared at Hockley dumbly, her knuckles white with the strength of her grip.

'Is that right, ma'am?' he asked again.

She moistened her lips quickly and nodded.

'Yes,' she said in a low, dry, whisper. 'Yes, that's — that's quite right.'

'Your first husband died in unfortunate circumstances,' went on Hockley. 'You were tried and acquitted for his murder . . .'

'Well, what about it?' broke in Conway harshly. 'Supposing she was? That was eleven years ago. What's the point in raking it all up? She was acquitted, wasn't she?'

'Oh yes,' answered the superintendent. 'I'm very sorry to have to bring the matter up, but there you are. It's my duty to confirm facts when they come into my possession . . . '

'How did you know?' asked Mrs. Conway, speaking with difficulty. 'Who — who told you?'

'I'm afraid, ma'am, I can't give you . . . '

'Was it someone in the village,' she broke in. 'Do they know about it?'

Hockley shook his head. He felt sorry for this woman whose face had gone so suddenly white and stricken.

'No,' he replied, 'and there's no reason why it should become public property at all. I've got to make these inquiries — you can't pick and choose when you're investigating a murder . . . '

'What has this got to do with Mrs. Mallaby's murder?' demanded Conway sharply.

'So far as I know, nothing,' admitted Hockley candidly. 'But I'm sure you'll realise, that in a matter of this sort, one can't be a respecter of persons. I'm checking up on everything an' everybody that might have some bearing on it.' He

161

was trying to be as pleasant over it as he could. He disliked the job, but it had to be done. 'Now when this information about you came to my ears, I had to make sure that it was correct, you see. You'll understand that, I'm sure.'

'Yes . . . I understand that,' muttered Mrs. Conway.

'Now you have made sure, what then?' asked her husband.

'Well, sir,' said Hockley, 'perhaps you could tell me whether anyone round here 'ud be likely to know about it? That your wife was named Lucas before she married you?'

'Nobody knew about it,' declared Conway, and he added bitterly: 'Though how long it will be before the whole village knows, I can't say.'

'They won't from me,' said Hockley quickly. 'I can assure you of that. Mrs. Mallaby wouldn't have known anything about it, would she?'

'I shouldn't think so,' answered Conway. 'She wouldn't have been able to keep a thing like that to herself. If you'd known her as well as we did, you wouldn't need to ask . . . '

'She would have taken a delight in spreading it all over the village,' whispered Mary under her breath. 'She was like that. She was responsible for more misery and unhappiness . . . '

'That'll do, dear,' interrupted her husband gently. 'She won't be responsible any more.'

Superintendent Hockley looked from one to the other of them, and rubbed his smooth chin. Were they quite ignorant of how Mrs. Mallaby had come by her death, or had they stopped that tongue of hers before it could do any damage? It was impossible to tell — yet.

He had confirmed Gould's statement about Mrs. Conway and there for the time being, he would have to leave it.

With a further apology for having disturbed them, he took his departure, and with him went peace . . .

★ ★ ★

'Do wake up, Peter,' said Margaret. 'You're being terribly rude.'

'Eh?' Peter opened his eyes and blinked at her from the depths of the settee. 'I wasn't asleep. I was thinking. I've always found that closing one's eyes is an aid to concentration.'

Ann laughed, and his sister uttered a derisive sound which was more expressive than polite.

'I suppose the weird noises you've been making is the mental machinery creaking?' she remarked sarcastically.

'Are you insinuating that I've been snoring?' he demanded, sitting up.

'No,' retorted Margaret, 'I'm stating a fact. Ask Ann.'

'You have, you know, Peter,' said Ann.

'I must have dropped off for a second,' said Peter, helping himself to a cigarette. 'I'm very sorry . . .'

'A second?' echoed Margaret scornfully. 'You've been snoring loudly for the last half-hour.' She held out the box of cigarettes to Ann, who shook her head. 'What I want to know is, when do you propose to start detecting?' she went on, taking a cigarette herself. 'You've done absolutely nothing yet.'

'That's where you're wrong,' declared Peter, lighting her cigarette and his own and throwing the used match in the fire. 'I've been analysing the situation.'

'We heard you,' said Ann, laughing.

'No, really, I have,' he said, blowing out a cloud of smoke toward the ceiling. 'It's going to be a very difficult job . . .'

'The Great Detective is completely baffled — before he's even started,' said Margaret.

'I wish you'd be quiet for a minute or two and let me talk,' exclaimed Peter. 'What I was going to say was, that it's going to be a very difficult job to get hold of all the facts. I can't go around questioning people like the brilliant amateur does in books. I should get chucked out.'

'Well, what are you going to do, then?' demanded his sister. 'Sit down and wait for the murderer to call and say: 'I did it, old boy?''

'No,' said Peter, 'but I can't make bricks without straw.'

'Why don't you be honest, Peter,' said Margaret, 'and admit that you took too big a bite and can't chew it?'

'Because that wouldn't be honest,' answered Peter. 'It wouldn't be the truth. I believe I can solve this mystery, once I'm in possession of the facts. Perhaps that sounds a bit silly, but what I mean is, that at the moment, I know so very little about it that I can't even start to theorise . . . '

'I know what you mean, Peter,' said Ann. 'All you know at the moment is that Mrs. Mallaby — I can't think of her as anything else — was killed in St. Mary's Church between four o'clock and half past last Friday afternoon . . . '

'That's all anyone knows,' interpolated Margaret.

'No, it isn't,' contradicted Peter. 'Hockley probably knows a great deal more. I've no doubt he's checked up on a number of people's alibis — in fact I know he has. He knew where the Conways were supposed to have been at the time. But I don't know where anybody was, and if I asked them, they'd tell me to mind my own business.'

'It doesn't look as if you were going to

get very far, does it?' said his sister cheerfully.

'Not that way,' said Peter. He got up and began to walk about the room aimlessly. 'However,' he went on, 'let's see how far we can get with what we *do* know. I think we should be pretty safe in saying that the murder was committed by a man.'

'Why?' asked Ann.

'The medical evidence suggested that the weapon was a penknife,' said Peter. 'Now, how many women carry penknives about with them?'

'I don't think that's a bit conclusive,' disagreed Margaret, shaking her head. 'For one thing they only said it might have been a penknife. There's no proof that it was. For another, if a woman had committed the crime, she could have taken the penknife with her to make people think it was a man.'

'That's possible,' admitted Peter.

'I'll have a cigarette now, if I may,' interrupted Ann. She reached forward and took one from the box on the table and Peter paused in his perambulation of the room to light it for her. 'Thanks.'

'So you see,' said Margaret triumphantly, 'you can't assume that the murderer was a man, after all.'

'But we can assume that it was someone with a pretty good knowledge of anatomy,' said Peter. 'The blow had to be instantly fatal. The murderer couldn't risk making a mistake over that. And it was quite a tricky thing to strike in exactly the right place. There's a lot of bony structure at the base of the skull and unless the exact spot had been found, the blade of the knife would have turned and Mrs. Mallaby would have started squealing like a stuck pig.'

'That's something, Peter,' exclaimed Ann. 'I shouldn't think many people would know the right spot.'

'It looks as though you'll have to arrest Boggs, the butcher,' said Margaret. 'He'd know . . .'

'So would Billing,' remarked Peter. 'He used to be a Scoutmaster . . .'

'You've always had an idea it was Billing, haven't you?' said his sister.

'I've kept the possibility in mind,' said

Peter cautiously. 'It would have been so easy for Billing — always supposing he had a motive. Going back to what we were talking about — the weapon. The knowledge of exactly where to strike is more likely to have been known to a man than to a woman. So, coupled with the fact that the weapon was probably a penknife, I think, for the sake of argument, we might assume that the murderer is a man.'

'All right, we'll assume that,' said Margaret. 'What then?'

'Then we'll see where it leads us,' continued Peter. He ticked off the various points on his fingers as he spoke: 'The murderer is a man. He is sufficiently acquainted with the construction of the human body to know exactly the spot where a wound in the nape of the neck, inflicted with a sharp instrument, like a penknife, will prove instantly fatal. He is also sufficiently acquainted with Mrs. Mallaby's habits to know that he will find her alone in the church for a few minutes on any afternoon in the vicinity of four o'clock. He is either someone who is in business on his own, or doesn't work at all . . . '

'Oh, look here, you can't assume that,' protested Margaret. 'Particularly that last bit. He might have had a day off, or been out on an errand, or anything.'

'All right,' said Peter resignedly, 'we'll leave out the last bit, if you like. But the rest of it is pretty sound . . . '

'The rest of it could apply to either a man or a woman,' said his sister.

'I think it was a man,' remarked Ann thoughtfully. 'It doesn't seem the sort of thing a woman would do. I don't mean that a woman wouldn't kill, I mean that she wouldn't do it *that* way. Surely it must have required a certain amount of strength?'

'Not more than a woman would possess,' said Peter. 'I thought of that. But I do agree with your other point. It's not the type of murder that a woman would choose. I think she'd try something more subtle . . . '

'Like poison?' said Ann, nodding. 'I'm sure you're right about that.'

'It would have been just as easy to plan

something like that,' said Peter, 'and that would have been the first thing to occur to a woman.'

'What makes you think it was planned at all?' asked Margaret. 'Why shouldn't it have been done on the spur of the moment?'

Peter shook his head.

'I don't think there's any doubt that it was planned,' he declared. 'I think that the murderer was waiting, hidden somewhere in the church, for Mrs. Mallaby to arrive.'

Ann gave a little shiver.

'It's rather horrible, isn't it?' she said almost in a whisper. 'Waiting there — until she had knelt down to pray . . . '

The front door bell rang loudly.

'I'll go,' said Peter. 'I wonder who the deuce it is.'

He crossed the hall and opened the front door. Three men, whom he recognised as reporters, stood on the step.

'It's no good,' said Peter quickly, before they had time to speak. 'I've got nothing to say . . . '

'We don't want to see you, Mr. Hunt,'

said one of them. 'There's a lady staying with you . . . '

'She's got nothing to say, either,' said Peter and started to shut the door.

'Hold on a minute, Mr. Hunt,' said the reporter who had spoken before. 'Is it true that Miss Lexford is the illegitimate daughter of the . . . '

'Good afternoon, gentlemen,' interrupted Peter firmly, and dexterously shut the door. 'Reporters,' he explained when he returned to the living-room. 'After your blood, Ann. I've got rid of 'em, but they'll try again. There's nothing quite so persistent as a reporter after a story . . . '

'Except a detective on the track of a murderer,' remarked his sister mischievously. 'Let's get on with the discussion, Peter.'

It didn't lead them very far, and when eventually Margaret got up with a yawn and suggested tea, they were no nearer to discovering the identity of Mrs. Mallaby's murderer than they had been when they started.

Ann Lexford received an anoymous letter by the first post on the following morning. It was full of abuse; an obscene and filthy document. She showed it to Peter and he immediately rang up Superintendent Hockley. Apparently she was not the only person who had been singled out for attention by the unknown scribe. The Reverend Mr. Popkiss, Miss Ginch and Hockley himself, had all been recipients of the anonymous writer's foul and illiterate scrawls.

8

Superintendent Hockley arrived at Peter's house in the middle of the following morning. He looked tired, harassed, and very worried. Peter took him up to his study and suggested a drink, which Hockley accepted with alacrity.

'I thought I'd better come and have a look at this letter,' he said, when he was ensconced in a deep armchair, and had been supplied with a large whisky and soda. 'There seems to be an epidemic of the things.'

'I have the letter here,' said Peter. 'Try one of these cigarettes?'

Hockley shook his head.

'Never smoke 'em, sir,' he said. 'Thanks all the same. A pipe's my mark, if you don't mind.'

'Go ahead,' said Peter, helping himself to a cigarette from the box on the littered desk, and lighting it. 'How's the investigation going?'

'Well, it is and it isn't, if you understand what I mean?' Hockley produced his battered pipe and began to fill it, slowly and methodically from his pouch. 'I'd like to have a word with Miss Lexford, if it's possible. That's really why I came along.'

'I'm sure she'll see you whenever you wish,' said Peter. 'She's downstairs with my sister. I'll call her.'

'Not just for the moment, sir, if you please,' said the superintendent. 'I'll have a look at that letter first.'

Peter took it from a drawer and pushed it across the desk.

'Do you think there's any connection between these things and the murder?' he asked.

'I don't know, sir,' said Hockley. 'You've got a queer sort of mentality responsible for these things, and you've got a queer sort of mentality responsible for the murder. They're both kinks an' there's no telling but what they mightn't be the same kink.'

He picked up the letter and read it through carefully.

'This is the same sort of muck as the others,' he said, laying the letter on his knee and lighting his pipe. 'She seems to use obscene words for the sheer delight in using 'em.'

'Why do you say 'she'?' asked Peter.

'It's nearly always a woman who goes in for this sort of thing, replied the superintendent. 'It's an outlet for some kind of sexual repression as a rule, an' you don't often find it in a man. Lor' bless you, sir, I've dealt with a lot of this kind of stuff in my time, and they were all written by women. I'm pretty sure these were too.'

'I think you're probably right,' agreed Peter, wondering how Hockley had acquired even this rudimentary knowledge of psychology.

'The trouble is,' Hockley continued, puffing at his pipe, 'there is no knowing where this sort o' kink will lead to. It's mental, you see, and there's no telling what turn it'll take. Even murder, sometimes.'

'It's my opinion,' said Peter, 'that the murder was committed by a man. I'll tell you why . . . '

He repeated what he had said to Ann and Margaret on the previous afternoon. Hockley listened interestedly.

'There's a good deal in what you say, sir,' he commented. 'In fact there's a lot in it — particularly about knowing the right place to strike. Now, who would you say would be likely to know that?'

Peter considered the question for a moment.

'Well,' he replied thoughtfully, scratching the bridge of his nose, 'there's Doctor Pratt, of course, and I suppose Boggs, the butcher, would know. Billing used to be a Scoutmaster, so I should think he'd know . . .'

'Billing was, was he?' said Hockley quickly. 'I've been wondering about Billing, sir.'

'So have I,' said Peter. 'Only what reason could he have had for killing Mrs. Mallaby?'

'I don't know, sir,' replied Hockley, 'but there's no getting away from the fact that he had the best opportunity of anyone. We've only his word for what happened in the church that afternoon, up to the time you appeared on the scene. I checked up on his movements and there's no saying but that he didn't get to the church much earlier than he said he did. He lives alone an' he could have done, without anyone being the wiser.'

'If only he had a motive,' said Peter.

'Maybe he had,' said the superintendent. 'Maybe it was something to do with this five hundred pounds that nobody seems to know anything about.'

'Five hundred pounds?' said Peter sharply. 'What five hundred pounds?'

'Ah, of course, you don't know anything about that, sir,' said Hockley. 'Well, it appears that the dead woman drew five hundred pounds all in one-pound notes, out of the bank on the Monday afternoon before her death. Up to the present, I can't find any reason why she did it, or any trace of the money . . . ' He related the full circumstances to the interested Peter. 'That's one of the reasons I wanted to see Miss Lexford, sir,' he concluded, 'I thought, perhaps, she might know something about it.'

'I'm quite sure she doesn't,' said Peter.

'If she did she'd have mentioned it. I say, you know, this looks remarkably like blackmail, doesn't it?'

'Yes, sir, it does — on the face of it,' agreed Hockley.

'I don't think there can be much doubt of it,' said Peter. He got up and began pacing the room excitedly. 'Why else should she have drawn this money all in pound notes? It must have been to pay somebody who had demanded it like that so that it couldn't be traced.'

'Yes, sir, but who?' said Superintendent Hockley. 'Who is the person who was blackmailing her, and what for? What did they know about her?'

'That's easy,' declared Peter. 'They knew the secret of Miss Lexford's birth.'

'I'll admit it sounds easy,' said Hockley, 'but when you come to work at it, sir, it's not so easy after all. Why did they wait all this long time before trying to cash in on what they knew . . . ?'

'Because,' broke in Peter, 'they *didn't* know before. They'd only just found out about it.'

'How?' demanded the superintendent.

'How did they only just find out? According to Miss Lexford only Mrs. Cooper knows anything about it.'

'Yes, that's true,' said Peter, and then as a thought struck him, 'I suppose Mrs. Mallaby didn't want this money for Mrs. Cooper?'

'She could have done,' said Hockley, nodding. 'I've already thought of that. I want Mrs. Cooper's address from Miss Lexford so that I can put through an inquiry.'

'Mrs. Mallaby would naturally send it in one-pound notes so that it couldn't be traced back to her,' said Peter.

'Maybe, sir,' said Hockley a trifle dubiously, 'but why did she send it at all? She'd never sent any large sum to Mrs. Cooper before, according to what Miss Lexford said. Why should she suddenly decide to do so? Unless, of course, it was Mrs. Cooper who was doing a bit of blackmail, and it seems a bit queer that she should have waited all this time to start that.'

'H'm,' grunted Peter. 'It does, doesn't it?'

He sat for a moment in frowning silence, while Hockley thoughtfully finished his whisky and soda. Suddenly he uttered an ejaculation.

'Look here,' he cried excitedly, 'there's one person who knew about Miss Lexford's birth whom we've forgotten.'

'Who's that, sir?' asked Hockley.

'Why, her father,' said Peter. 'Nobody knows who *he* was. She doesn't know. Mrs. Cooper doesn't know. Only Mrs. Mallaby knew . . . '

'That's an idea, sir,' exclaimed Hockley. 'I hadn't thought of that. You mean this five hundred quid may have been given to him?'

'Why not?' said Peter, striding up and down and frowning furiously. 'Or it might have been somebody who was closely associated with him. Somebody who knew about the affair . . . '

'I believe you've hit on something there, sir,' declared the superintendent. 'It's a possibility, anyhow. I don't see how it could have led to *her* murder. Now, if it was the other way round . . . '

'It could have led to her murder,' said

Peter. 'We don't know anything about this man. He may be respectably married now, with children, for all we know. I should think it was more than likely. Suddenly, for some reason or other, he finds himself hard pressed for money. He gets in touch with Mrs. Mallaby, and suggests that she should let him have the money he wants, hinting that it would be a pity if this youthful peccadillo of hers should become known.

'She agrees to let him have the money and arranges a meeting in the church for the Friday afternoon, in the meanwhile drawing out the cash from the bank. But she was a very mean woman and the thought of parting with all that money for nothing worries her. She makes a few inquiries about her erstwhile lover and learns that it would do him as much harm if the facts of the child's birth become public as it would her and flatly refuses to hand over a penny. He realises that his bluff has been called — he had never had any intention of really making the affair public — but he's desperate for money. He kills her and takes the five hundred pounds. How's that?'

'Very ingenious, sir,' remarked Hockley a trifle dryly. 'It does credit to your imagination, but from a practical point of view there are rather a lot of snags . . . '

'I don't see any that can't be got over,' said Peter, who had been rather proud of his theory, and was, in consequence, a little dampened by the superintendent's lukewarm reception of it. 'Tell me the snags.'

Hockley pressed down the burning tobacco in his pipe with an apparently asbestos finger.

'First,' he said thoughtfully. 'Do you think that this man would have suddenly decided on blackmail, after all this time? Particularly if, as you suggest, he'd got married an' had a family. He would think twice before stirring up the past . . . '

'He could be pretty certain that she wouldn't want it known,' said Peter. 'From his point of view there wasn't much risk.'

'I think there'd be more risk than he'd care to take,' said Hockley. 'That is if he was respectably married, as you suggest.

And if he isn't your whole theory falls to the ground.'

'H'm, well . . . What are your other objections?' asked Peter.

'It seems unlikely to me, sir,' replied Hockley, 'that Mrs. Mallaby, if she'd made this appointment for Friday, would have drawn the money such a long time ahead. She'd have waited until the Thursday, or even the Friday morning. And then again, if she'd waited until then she wouldn't have drawn it out at all because she'd made up her mind not to pay it over.'

Peter admitted the point of this.

'Also, sir,' continued Hockley, 'she was in a great hurry to draw the money. She hadn't got her cheque book with her and she got a single cheque from the bank. If she'd had until Friday she would have used one from her own book. There's one other point,' he added quickly, as Peter opened his mouth to speak, 'She was kneeling when she was killed. How could this man have got her to do that, if they'd just had a quarrel?'

Peter saw his theory thoroughly demolished and shrugged his shoulders.

'I admit the logic of your objections,' he said. 'All the same, I think it's very likely this unknown man may have something to do with the matter.'

'So do I, sir,' said Hockley, 'and I'm very much obliged for the suggestion. It's going to be a bit difficult to find him, after all this time, but I'll have inquiries made. The trouble is we don't know anything about him at all. We might get a clue if we can trace the dead woman's history back to the time she was in service. But it's not going to be easy.' He sighed and looked into the bowl of his pipe. 'If in some way, Billing could have found out about the child's birth now, it 'ud be pretty plain sailing . . .'

'You're up against as many snags there as you are with my idea, said Peter. 'More. Why should Billing, if he'd discovered a profitable source of income, kill the goose and put a stop to it for good. It's not even sense.'

'Perhaps she threatened to go to the police?' suggested the superintendent, but his tone was uncertain.

'Rubbish,' declared Peter scornfully. 'If she'd been going to the police she wouldn't have paid anything. In which case she wouldn't have drawn out the money. I wish we could see some way for Billing to have had a motive. I'm rather partial to him as the murderer . . . '

'I can't see what, sir,' said Hockley. 'He had the best opportunity and that's about all. By the way, that information from Gould was quite correct. I've checked up on it. Mrs. Conway admits that she was Mrs. Lucas.'

'I sincerely hope the fact won't leak out,' said Peter fervently. 'Her life won't be worth living, if it does. I don't think she had anything to do with this business.'

'I'm inclined to agree with you, sir,' said Hockley. 'But you can't tell — not in a case like this. Anybody might be guilty. There's just nothing, at the moment, to give us a lead. I shan't say anything about Mrs. Conway. I don't want to make trouble for anyone — except the person who killed Mrs. Mallaby. Could I see Miss Lexford now?'

Peter called Ann. She came readily and answered all Hockley's questions to the best of her ability. She knew nothing whatever about the five hundred pounds, and was convinced that Mrs. Cooper didn't, either. She had already written to Mrs. Cooper telling her of the murder and asking her to forward all Mrs. Mallaby's letters which she wanted to give to Mr. Buncombe. She had no information at all regarding the identity of her father, and neither, she was sure, had Mrs. Cooper. They had often discussed it but to no purpose. It was a secret known only to Mrs. Mallaby and the man concerned.

Hockley thanked her, stowed the anymous letter away in his wallet, and took his departure. He had an interview that afternoon with the Chief Constable and he was not looking forward to it.

The Chief Constable would want to hear what progress he had made with the case and he had practically nothing to report.

★   ★   ★

The funeral took place that afternoon. Mr. Buncombe had arranged everything, and he was the only mourner in the solitary coach that followed the hearse, and his was the only wreath on the resplendent coffin.

The Reverend Mr. Popkiss did not officiate, delegating that duty to his curate. There was a chill wind blowing, and as the coffin was lowered into the open grave, it began to rain . . .

★   ★   ★

'I wish,' said Mrs. Popkiss, pouring her husband out a second cup of tea, 'that I knew what was the matter with Olive.'

'What do you mean, m'dear?' asked her husband, inserting a large portion of buttered scone into his small mouth and wiping his fingers delicately on his handkerchief.

'Really, you never notice anything,' said Mrs. Popkiss irritably.

'I haven't noticed that there was anything wrong with Olive,' said Mr. Popkiss mildly, the hot scone making his speech a trifle difficult. 'What *is* the matter with her?'

'She's getting most peculiar,' said Mrs. Popkiss. 'So moody and morose. I really cannot understand what has come over her.'

'Perhaps,' suggested her husband, helping himself to another toasted scone, 'that her system is a little out of order. A dose of — er — Epsom salts or castor oil would, no doubt, put the matter right.'

'I don't think that's the cause of the trouble,' said Mrs. Popkiss.

'Where is she now?' asked the vicar.

'She went out after lunch. She hasn't come back yet,' answered his wife.

'Out?' The Reverend Mr. Popkiss looked at the window against which the rain was pattering noisily. 'Dear me, she should not be out on a wet day like this. Unless, of course, she has gone to visit some friend . . . ?'

'I don't know where she's gone,' said Mrs. Popkiss, smoothing the flat bosom of her black dress. 'And that is another thing. She has developed a strange kind of secretiveness lately. She goes out quite a lot but she never says where she has been . . . '

'Have you asked her?' said Mr. Popkiss.

'Of course I've asked her,' snapped his wife testily. 'She is merely evasive. All she says is that she's been for a walk.'

'May that not be the truth?' said the vicar, reaching for a piece of fruit cake.

'I cannot understand why she should have suddenly developed this desire for exercise,' said Mrs. Popkiss doubtfully. 'She always used to hate walking . . . '

'We change our habits as we grow older,' said Mr. Popkiss. 'I cannot think that Olive is doing anything that she ought not to be doing. It would grieve me very greatly to think so.'

He shook his head gravely.

'I'm not suggesting that,' said Mrs. Popkiss crossly. 'I'm only drawing your attention to something which I think you ought to know.' She sipped her tea elegantly. 'When she is not out she spends her time mooning about in her room. That is also something she never used to do.'

'I will speak to her,' said Mr. Popkiss. 'I

fear that I have not given sufficient attention to these domestic matters, m'dear. The parish has occupied a great deal of my time, especially since this — er — terrible upset over Mrs. Mallaby.'

'I don't see how it has affected you very much,' said Mrs. Popkiss acidly.

'It has distressed me beyond measure,' said the vicar, taking another piece of cake. 'Beyond measure,' he repeated.

'I never did like the Mallaby woman,' declared Mrs. Popkiss. 'I always thought there was something deceitful about her. I am not the least surprised to hear what she was.'

'It behoves us to think the best of people,' replied the vicar with a sigh, though whether it was the result of sorrow at the duplicity of the dead Mrs. Mallaby, or the very large tea he had consumed, was known only to himself. 'It is better to be deceived than distrusting. She has suffered a terrible penalty for her sin — a terrible penalty. The mills of God grind slowly, but they grind exceeding small.'

'I wonder who killed her?' asked Mrs.

Popkiss, not very impressed with this sentiment. Familiarity, if it had not actually bred contempt, had engendered something so much akin to it that the difference was negligible.

'That is not for us to conjecture,' said the vicar. 'The brand of Cain is, unfortunately, not a visible brand but is burnt indelibly upon the soul . . . '

'I suppose,' continued his wife, ignoring the brand of Cain, 'that the estate will go to this woman — what's-her-name — Lexford?'

'Presumably,' agreed the vicar, passing his cup for more tea. 'Most probably. Unless there is a will disposing of it otherwise.'

'It wouldn't surprise me,' said Mrs. Popkiss, pouring out the tea, 'if this woman hadn't had a great deal to do with the murder.'

Mr. Popkiss looked shocked.

'My dear,' he protested. Is it charitable to attribute actions to people, however debased they may be, for which there is no basis of proof?'

'Oh rubbish,' snapped his wife crossly.

'There's no harm in discussing these things amongst ourselves. It seems to me that, if there was no will, she had the greatest possible motive for doing it. If I were the police I should have put her under lock and key at once, instead of allowing her to flaunt herself about the neighbourhood. She must be completely shameless to appear in public at all, considering the stigma attaching to her birth.'

'I'm sure the police know very well what they are doing,' remarked Mr. Popkiss, adding another lump of sugar to his tea and stirring it gently. 'I think we may safely leave the matter to them, m'dear.'

Mrs. Popkiss wrinkled her long, thin, reddish nose and sniffed disparagingly. She would have replied if at that moment the door had not opened abruptly to admit Olive. She was dressed in a shabby raincoat and a close-fitting oilskin hat, both of which were streaming with water.

'Don't come in here like that,' greeted her mother sharply. 'Look at the mess you're making of the carpet. Go and take

193

your wet things off at once . . . '

'I want some tea,' said Olive sullenly.

'Then you should come home at the proper time,' said Mrs. Popkiss. 'Tea cannot be kept about to suit your convenience. Where have you been?'

'For a walk,' answered the girl shortly.

'Surely,' said her father, 'the weather is a little inclement for walking?'

'It's as good as any other weather,' said Olive. She looked tired and exhausted, although her restless eyes were very bright. 'Can I have a cup of tea?'

'You'll have to fetch some more hot water,' said Mrs. Popkiss, holding out the jug. 'And take those wet things off at the same time,' she added.

Olive took the jug and went out without a word.

'I can't think what's come over her,' said Mrs. Popkiss, shaking her head. 'Her behaviour is most strange.'

'I will seek an opportunity of talking to her,' said the vicar. He rose ponderously to his feet and pulled down his waistcoat. 'But not now. I must go and prepare my sermon.'

He sailed majestically from the room, ascended to his comfortable study, settled himself in a deep easy-chair before the fire, and was soon dozing peacefully, oblivious to all extraneous matters.

★　★　★

'Wake up,' whispered Mrs. Popkiss, nudging her husband with a sharp elbow. 'Wake up!'

Mr. Popkiss stirred in the large bed, like a whale roused from sleep, and opened his eyes to utter darkness.

'Wake up!' hissed his wife again.

'I am awake,' he answered resentfully. 'What's the matter?'

'Sh-s-s,' she whispered warningly. 'There's somebody moving about in the house. Get up and see who it is.'

'You've been dreaming,' began Mr. Popkiss, annoyed at the disturbance of his slumbers, but she interrupted him.

'I have not been dreaming,' she declared in the same low, urgent whisper. 'There is somebody moving about in the house. I heard them. Perhaps it's Agnes . . . '

Agnes was their one small, rather overworked servant.

Mr. Popkiss stared up into the darkness, listening.

'I can't hear anything,' he said.

'Get up,' urged his wife.

The vicar sighed and resignedly hoisted himself out of his warm bed. Switching on the shaded lamp on the small table by the bed-head, he pulled on his dressing-gown and thrust his feet into slippers. A glance at the table clock showed him that it was just on two and, in confirmation of this, the hour struck from the tower of the church nearby. He listened again but could hear nothing. The house appeared to be quite silent.

'You must have been mistaken,' he muttered, but Mrs. Popkiss, now sitting up in bed with an eiderdown round her skinny shoulders, shook her head.

'I distinctly heard somebody moving about,' she said. 'Go and see, but go quietly or they'll hear you.'

Reluctantly, he went over to the door and opened it. The passage into which he peered was quite dark and not in the least inviting. The dim ray from the lamp in the bedroom fell in a broad stripe on the opposite wall, in the centre of which his shadow loomed up vague and monstrous.

Listening, he heard a faint sound from the direction of the staircase leading down to the hall: an unmistakable creak from one of the treads.

Pulling the bedroom door to behind him, and shutting off the streak of dim light, he stood in the darkness of the corridor and listened again. There was a second faint creak. Somebody was stealthily ascending or descending the stairs.

As noiselessly as he could, he moved along the wall towards the landing, guiding himself with the tips of outstretched fingers. There was a switch at the end of the passage which put the light on in the hall below and would illumine the staircase revealing the person who was up and about at this hour.

He reached the landing and groped for the switch in the dark. After a little while he found it and pressed it down. The darkness fled as the light came on, like the sudden whisking away of an enveloping cloak.

Before him the broad stairway stretched downwards to the hall, and near the foot of it, pressed back against the wall, as though hoping by that very pressure she would merge with it and become invisible, was Olive.

She was fully dressed with a coat wrapped round her thick, shapeless body and a scarf covering her hair. With her mouth drooping open and her eyes wide and dilated with fear, she stared up at her father.

'Olive!' he exclaimed. 'What is the meaning of this? What are you doing dressed like that at this hour of the night?'

She said nothing — only stared at him dumbly.

'Where were you going?' demanded the vicar, advancing to the head of the stair. 'You were going out. Where were you going?'

Still she made no answer. No sound or movement of any sort. Only that blank stare.

The Reverend Mr. Popkiss slowly

descended the stairs. His eyes were stern and accusing; his mouth compressed.

'Will you explain the meaning of this?' he said, stopping in front of her. 'Where were you going?'

She moved for the first time, a shrinking movement as though she expected a blow. Her lips moved too, a queer twitching spasm, like St. Vitus dance.

But still she said nothing.

'Have you lost your tongue?' demanded her father angrily. 'I insist upon an immediate explanation of your conduct, Olive.'

For a moment there was no change in her expression. And then, suddenly, she began to laugh. She became convulsed with laughter so that her ungainly shoulders shook. But it was a strange, inward, secretive laughter that was almost completely silent. There was something horrible about it, horrible and malignant.

'Olive,' cried the vicar sharply. 'Olive, what is the matter with you?'

But Olive only continued to laugh until the tears were running down her fat cheeks.

'Do you hear me,' exclaimed Mr. Popkiss, rather alarmed. 'Stop that at once . . . '

In his exasperation he caught her by the arm and shook her. Something white dropped from under her coat and fell on the stairs; three letters that scattered as they fell to form an accusing semi-circle.

The vicar stooped and picked them up. They were all stamped and addressed in an illiterate, printed hand . . .

He stared at them in incredulous horror.

'*You* wrote these?' he whispered hoarsely. 'You wrote these . . . You were going out to post them . . . '

She turned on him, swiftly and unexpectedly. There issued from her lips a stream of the filthiest invective. And then she began to laugh again, not silently as before, but with a great hysterical outburst that went echoing, like the laughter of a thousand devils, through the stillness of the house . . .

9

'Have you 'eard the news?' demanded Mr. Muncher, bursting breathlessly into the bar at the Fox and Hounds just after it had opened. 'Olive Popkiss 'as gone balmy!'

Mr. Penny, and the customers who were sampling his excellent beer, greeted this statement with frank disbelief.

'It's a fact,' declared Mr. Muncher. 'I 'ad it from the gardener a few seconds ago. Went balmy durin' the night, she did. They've sent for a specialist from Lun'un . . .'

* * *

'Have you heard about Olive Popkiss?' said Miss Dewsnap to Miss Ginch, later in the day. 'Quite out of her mind, poor thing.'

'Yes, indeed,' replied Miss Ginch, shaking her head sorrowfully. 'My heart bleeds for the dear vicar.'

'I always thought that Olive was — well, a little peculiar,' remarked Miss Dewsnap, who had done nothing of the kind. 'I've heard that she was responsible for all those dreadful letters, too . . . '

'Really, I can scarcely believe that,' said Miss Ginch. 'Where could she have learned all those very objectionable words — I didn't know the meaning of some of them.'

'They say she wrote them, all the same,' affirmed Miss Dewsnap.

★   ★   ★

' . . . tried to kill her father with the bread-knife,' said Colonel Bramber. 'Mad as a hatter. Shockin' thing.'

'We might all have been killed in our beds,' said Mrs. Bramber, popping a large piece of Turkish delight into her mouth. 'Really, there always seems to be something unpleasant happening lately. We never had anything of the sort in India . . . '

★   ★   ★

'I should think that living with the Popkisses would be enough to drive anyone mad,' remarked Diana Withers. 'Not that Olive had to be driven very far. She was always halfway there.'

'Miss Dewsnap told me she was dancing in the hall in the nude,' said her mother with great relish.

'That must have been a charming sight,' said Diana.

*   *   *

'There's no doubt at all but that she did write those letters,' said Superintendent Hockley to Sergeant Tripp. 'Apart from the ones found on her at the vicarage when her father discovered her in the hall, there were several partly finished ones locked in a drawer in her bedroom. Sort of drafts, I suppose, which she hadn't used.'

'Well, I'd never have believed it,' declared Tripp, scratching his head. 'Fancy a girl like that knowing all them words — and a parson's daughter at that. Beats me where she got hold of 'em.'

'It surprised me a bit,' admitted Hockley, 'though it shouldn't have done, really. After all, she's just the type who would write that muck. Suppressed, narrow life, warped outlook, no excitement . . . Doctor Pratt says she must have been on the borderline of a mental breakdown for some time. I suppose the shock of being caught by her father in the act, as you might say, tipped the balance.'

'What'll they do with her?' asked Tripp curiously, transferring his scratching operation by easy stages from his head to his ear and thence to his nose.

'Depends a lot, I should say, on what the specialist says when he's examined her,' said Hockley. 'Maybe he'll recommend putting her in a home for a bit. With proper attention she might recover. It's pretty bad luck on her parents.'

'Well, I should say it was a good deal their fault,' said the sergeant. 'Something wrong about her bringing up, if you ask me. Young people have got to have an outlet — it's only natural. Look at my girl Jenny. Pictures an' dances, pictures an' dances; every night it's one or the other — an' boys . . . Why they're always hanging about the 'ouse. But there ain't no harm in her. You wouldn't find a better nor a nicer girl not in a day's march, though I says it as shouldn't.'

'I'm sure you wouldn't,' agreed Superintendent Hockley.

★ ★ ★

'Peter, do you think that this girl, Olive Popkiss, could have . . . ?' Ann stopped and he finished the sentence for her.

'Committed the murder, do you mean?' he said. 'Yes, I think she could quite easily. Except for one thing. It wouldn't explain that five hundred pounds.'

'Is there any need to explain that?' she asked quickly. 'I mean, it might have nothing at all to do with the murder, after all.'

'No,' said Peter thoughtfully, 'but it would be tidier, somehow, if we could fit it in.'

She smiled.

'You feel like that because you are

used to working out plots,' she said, 'and you like to round them off neatly. But life isn't tidy or neat, Peter. It's full of what you call loose ends. People do things on impulse that sometimes can't be accounted for.'

'You're quite right, of course,' agreed Peter. 'The murder could quite possibly be an extension of the mental disorder which drove Olive Popkiss to write those letters. In which case, of course, there would be no motive — not the usual cut and dried one, that is.' He lit a cigarette and frowned at the glowing end. 'But I'm not really satisfied with that explanation, you know,' he continued after a pause. 'You can say it's the novelist's mind, if you like, but I'm sure that five hundred pounds is at the root of the matter. In fact, I'm convinced that if we could find out what happened to that, everything else would become automatically clear.'

'Well, if we are going to find out the truth before I go,' said Ann, 'we've got to work pretty quickly. I've got to go back on Sunday.'

'I know,' said Peter. 'I wish you hadn't.

Only three full days and a bit.' He sighed. 'Perhaps I shall get a brainwave before then.'

* * *

The mental specialist arrived from London on the Thursday afternoon to see Olive Popkiss, and after careful examination and a number of exhaustive tests, gave it as his considered opinion that there was a slight chance of her recovering normality if she underwent a course of treatment and was placed under constant supervision.

This would necessitate, indeed it was essential, that she should be removed from her present and familiar surroundings at the earliest possible moment.

There was a sanatorium, run by the specialist himself, for cases of her description. It was expensive, but the specialist thought that he could arrange for her admittance. If she went there she would, of course, be under his own personal care.

The Reverend Mr. Popkiss, more disturbed than he had ever been in the whole of his rather uneventful life, agreed. The specialist telephoned the Home and everything was suitably arranged.

A nurse would come on the following day and take the patient back with her. In the meanwhile, Olive was not to be left alone for a single minute. These cases were often unpredictable and she might try and do herself an injury.

The specialist shook hands genially with the anxious and worried Mr. Popkiss and departed, carrying with him a large cheque.

The newspaper reporters seized upon the matter as manna sent from heaven. The murder, which was their legitimate reason for being in Long Manton at all, had hung fire and their various news editors were getting a little impatient. Here was something to offer as a sop until more sensational news came along.

Therefore, they besieged the vicarage and pestered everybody who might, even remotely, be expected to add some small item to their information.

Peter, coming down into the village for a supply of cigarettes, ran unexpectedly into Superintendent Hockley and inquired how the investigation was going.

'Well, sir,' answered Hockley, who was looking a trifle depressed, 'I'm following up all the lines I've got. The local police are dealing with Mrs. Cooper and I'm expecting a report from them at any moment. Otherwise . . . ' He shrugged his shoulders expressively.

'Otherwise nothing, eh?' said Peter. 'You've heard nothing more of the five hundred pounds?'

Hockley shook his head.

'Nothing at all,' he said.

'Well, the source of the anonymous letters has been cleared up,' remarked Peter. 'That's something. You haven't got to worry about that any more — unless you think that Olive's madness may have taken a more serious turn.'

'It's something I've got to take into account, sir,' said the superintendent seriously, 'and if it should be the truth, it looks as if this murder'll remain one of the unsolved crimes, because there doesn't seem much chance of bringing it home to her.'

'Have you found out where she was on the Friday afternoon?' asked Peter. 'If she has an alibi . . . '

'She hasn't,' answered Hockley a little shortly. 'I didn't overlook that. She was out that afternoon, like she was on most afternoons recently. She used to spend hours wandering about by herself. Nobody seems to know where she went or what she did.'

'I suppose you had a word with the specialist?' said Peter. 'What was his opinion? Did he think it likely she could have turned homicidal?'

'He thought it was unlikely,' replied Hockley. 'But he wouldn't commit himself definitely one way or the other.'

'Well, I don't think that's the solution, anyway,' declared Peter. 'I don't think it was Olive. There's a much more practical explanation — one that includes that five hundred pounds.'

'I wish,' said Hockley fervently, 'that I could find it.'

The superintendent went on his way, and Peter, continuing along the High Street, turned into the tobacconists and bought his cigarettes. They had run out of hundred boxes and Peter had to take his supply in packets of twenty, which for some reason or other, for he was usually fairly easy-going, annoyed him.

He came out of the shop in a bad temper and set out to walk back to his house. He wondered what it was that was making him feel so irritable and discovered, rather to his surprise, that it was because Ann would be leaving so soon.

The thought was unpleasant and depressing.

He had had a fair sprinkling of love affairs in his time, some of them transient, some of longer duration, but none of the women had ever affected him in quite the same way that Ann did.

The emotions that she stirred up within him defied analysis, or perhaps it was these very emotions themselves that prevented him applying it properly.

Passion? Desire? . . . Yes, they were there in full measure, but they had been there with the others. They had been the beginning and the end. They had not been off-shoots, as it were, of this other something — this great flooding emotion that welled up within him, whenever he thought of Ann, and drowned everything but herself.

This was a new experience. This had never happened to him before.

He was not giving to her the crust of his mind but the whole of it, and, with it, his soul and body and everything that was essentially *he*.

From the moment when she had walked into the drawing-room at Manton Lodge, he had instinctively known this. He realised that now, although he had not entirely realised it then.

He had imagined, then, that it was because she was the living prototype of the girl in his book, on the creation of whom he had lavished so much thought and care. It had never occurred to him that he had epitomised in the fictional character of April every attribute that constituted his idea of the ideal woman.

And this ideal of his fancy had come suddenly to life.

It was rather like Pygmalion and Galatea all over again.

It turned out to be a sunny, warm afternoon and Peter suggested, after lunch, that they should go for a walk.

Margaret declined, offering as an excuse that she had several jobs to do in the house, and a lot of letters to write, that couldn't be put off any longer. So Ann and Peter went together.

He took her through the woods behind the house and out into open country. Below them sprawled the village, in a hollow, surrounded by all the sad beauty of autumn.

'It's very lovely here, you know, Peter,' said Ann as they turned into a hedge-lined lane scored by wheel tracks.

'I think so,' he answered. 'You should see it in the spring when all the fresh green is bursting. You can almost feel the pressure of life in everything — a great upsurge of renewed energy. That's my favourite time of the year, I think, though all the seasons have a charm.'

'I love the country,' said Ann.

'Yes. There's always something exciting

about it,' said Peter. 'In a town you see the same streets and the same shops; the same houses and buildings. But the country's always different. You seem to be constantly coming upon a view, an aspect, that you never quite saw in the same way before. Of course, the fields and the footpaths, the woods and the lanes don't change their positions any more than the streets and the buildings in a town do, but they seem to acquire a variety . . . I don't know how to explain what I mean exactly. It's something that you can't put into words properly. You can only feel it.'

'I know what you mean,' said Ann quickly. 'It's because nearly everything in the country is *living*. In the town it's dead . . . '

'I think you've hit it,' he said. 'Yes, that's what you feel in the country. Life and change — going on all around you. Not the life and change of the streets but something more fundamental. The life and change of nature.'

They came out of the lane and struck across a footpath.

'You are a lover of the country, Ann,'

said Peter after a short silence, 'and yet you live the greater part of your life in London.'

'That's from necessity,' she answered, 'not from choice.'

'Do you like your work?' he asked.

'Yes, I do, very much indeed. It's interesting. I thoroughly enjoy it. I don't think I could ever do a job just for the money I got out of it.'

'I don't think I could,' said Peter. 'Yet there are thousands of people who have to.'

'And there are likely to be thousands more, as things are going,' she said. 'The machine age, with its inevitable standardisation of nearly everything, has killed the old, individual love of craftsmanship, the joy of making something really well for its own sake.'

'More's the pity,' said Peter. 'Beauty is rapidly fading before progress. Everything is cut to a pattern. Thousands of this; millions of that, all exactly alike, products of the assembly belt. And houses, too. Look at the new towns, growing like mushrooms or weeds, sprawling over the countryside. Whole streets of houses, like so many jellies in a mould. And the people are getting like the products they help to make. Taken as a mass there is very little individuality left nowadays. They look alike, think alike — an army of robots.'

'What else can you expect?' said Ann. 'If you spend your days endlessly putting one little screw into a hole ready drilled for it by somebody else who does nothing but drill little holes, how can you acquire anything like individuality? You don't have to think. You can have neither pride nor interest in the finished article. It's not a creation of your hand or brain. Hundreds of people have contributed their own particular little portion to it. You are bound to become an automaton.'

'And the joy of the craftsman is nearly gone,' said Peter. 'They work with one eye on the clock, waiting for the time when work shall be over and they can take their leisure. And here again they've lost the power to really enjoy themselves. They don't have to make amusement any more. Their leisure is almost an extension of the same system as their work. A standardised entertainment. The same films, the same dance numbers, the same television programmes — a constant hotchpotch of the same plots under different titles . . . '

'But if you gave them something different, Peter, they wouldn't like it . . . '

'No,' he answered quickly, 'because their minds have become standardised too. They've lost the power to think for themselves. There was a time when they had to seek their own amusement, make it. Now everything's handed to them on a plate and their minds have become atrophied . . . '

'The graciousness of life has gone,' said Ann.

He turned his head towards her quickly.

'Yes,' he said, 'that's really true. The graciousness of life *has* gone and I'm very much afraid it will never come back. You can see the fading sparks of it sometimes in old people; people who remember a period of good manners and courtesy. But now, more's the pity, there's no time for all that. Life has speeded up. How quickly can one get from here to there and back again. The jet age, the rocket age. Not content with having made a complete and utter mess of the earth, man is now set upon doing the same thing with the planets. The space age. Beauty and peace mean nothing any more. The loveliness of dawn, the still tranquillity of a summer evening, what do they matter compared to shrieking through space at a speed faster than sound? There is so much that could be done to make life more pleasant on this beautiful earth instead of seeking new worlds.'

'You don't believe in progress?' she asked.

'Is it progress?' said Peter. 'The hydrogen bomb, capable of wiping out whole countries — is that progress? Is that the goal of civilisation? To fill the sky with noise and man-made satellites — is that progress? If it is then I am against it. Civilisation is really a myth. Very few people are really civilised. They are covered with a veneer of civilisation but it is very thin and liable to peel off at the slightest provocation. Look at the gangs of Teddy-boys with their razors and bicycle chains. Read every day the cruelty to children by their parents, brutal, bestial cruelty. The old savage instincts are scarcely even sleeping. Good plumbing and chromium plate don't make civilisation. They only surround the savage with better comforts than a mud hut.'

They came to a stile and he helped her over. The footpath continued on the other side and struck off across open fields. Somewhere near at hand, the smoke from a bonfire of leaves rose greyly into the still air, and the acrid tang of it reached them.

Ann sighed.

'I shall be sorry to go back,' she said. 'It's lovely here. Quiet and peaceful.'

'Very,' said Peter with a twinkle in his eye. 'A murder and a lunatic. Peace, perfect peace.'

'You know very well what I mean,' she said. 'None of those things make any difference to this.' She waved an arm around.

'No, there's nothing sordid about the country, is there?' said Peter. 'No matter what *people* do. I shall be sorry when you go, Ann.'

They walked on for a moment or two in silence. Then she said:

'You know, Peter, we're not getting very far with our detection, are we?'

'I'm afraid we're not,' he answered. He had been thinking of something that was very far from the murderer of Mrs. Mallaby. 'If we could only find out what has happened to the five hundred pounds. I'm sure that's the key to the puzzle. I've thought so ever since I heard about it.'

'If the police can't find out, I don't see how we can,' said Ann. 'They have far more facilities than we have.'

'There must be some trace of it somewhere,' said Peter. 'Five hundred pounds in pound notes can't just vanish away . . .'

'It can be spent, which comes to the same thing,' replied Ann. 'Who could she had paid it to and why?'

'The why wouldn't matter if we only knew who,' muttered Peter. 'She drew the money out of the bank on Monday and we've no proof that she didn't send, or give it away on the same day . . . '

'I should think she probably did,' said Ann. 'She must have been in a violent hurry for it, or she wouldn't have used a cheque form instead of a cheque from her own book . . . '

Peter frowned.

'Which looks,' he said, 'as if she didn't expect to need this money when she started out from home on that Monday. Otherwise she would have written out the cheque before she left and taken it with her. I never thought of that before . . . '

'You mean,' she said quickly, 'that the need for this money came suddenly, between the time she left Manton Lodge and the time she reached the bank?'

'It looks like it,' said Peter.

'Which means that she must have met somebody on the way,' she said.

'Somebody who made her see the immediate necessity of paying them five hundred pounds?' remarked Peter. 'How did they do it?'

'Blackmail,' said Ann.

'Yes, but what for?' said Peter. 'And did she pay the money on the Monday . . . '

'She must have,' broke in Ann, 'or she wouldn't have been in such a hurry to get it.'

'And having got her five hundred pounds,' said Peter, 'the person, whoever it was, waited till the Friday and then killed her. Why?'

'It seems to be nothing but why?' said Ann plaintively.

'I'm afraid that seems to be as far as we get,' he agreed. 'It's possible, of course, that this person got the five hundred pounds under some form of false pretences, and he was afraid that Mrs. Mallaby would discover it . . . '

'If only we could find out who she met,' said Ann. 'Surely someone must have seen them . . . '

'Hockley would have covered that line of inquiry,' said Peter. 'If anyone *had* seen her with anybody they would have come forward.'

He stopped suddenly in the middle of the footpath.

'What's the matter?' asked Ann in surprise.

'She would have gone into the church

on the Monday, like she always did, wouldn't she?' said Peter. 'No, that's no good. That would have been after she drew the money.'

'You were thinking that she might have met this person in the church?' she asked, and he nodded.

'Yes, but it would have been too late,' he replied. He was facing her as she stood looking at him, her eyes questioning and her lips slightly parted with expectancy. Something that was completely beyond his control and acted without any conscious volition of his own took possession of Peter then.

Without a word he stepped forward and his arms went round her. He felt her yield to his embrace with a sudden eagerness that surprised him.

'Ann,' he whispered in a voice that was husky with emotion. 'Ann . . . I love you . . . I've loved you from the moment you walked into that room at Manton Lodge . . . Will you marry me?'

She looked up at him. Her eyes were shining, but there was a faint twitching at the corners of her lips.

'What are you laughing at?' he demanded suspiciously.

'Well, it was . . . it was rather sudden, wasn't it?' she said. 'I don't want to sound like the — the . . . '

But what she was going to say was muffled by Peter's lips and for a long time she could say nothing, even if she'd wanted to. When eventually his lips had reluctantly freed themselves, she said in a voice that shook a little:

'I — I don't remember Sherlock Holmes ever doing *that* to Doctor Watson, do you . . . ?'

10

Margaret had tea ready by a quarter to five. At half past five, when there was still no sign of Peter and Ann, she had her tea and settled down with a book and a cigarette.

They did not put in an appearance until half past six, by which time it was completely dark.

'I expected you hours ago,' said Margaret. 'Where have you been? I hope you've had tea somewhere . . .'

'We've not had tea,' said Peter, 'but we'd like some. Don't you bother, though, I'll make it.'

'No, let me,' said Ann, taking off the coat she had borrowed from Margaret.

'But where have you been?' demanded Margaret. 'Surely to goodness you haven't been walking all this time?'

'Well, not exactly all the time,' replied Peter. 'We sat down for a rest on that fallen tree by the stile in Burton's fields and we didn't notice how late it was getting . . . '

His sister eyed him critically.

'H'm, I see,' she said, nodding slowly. 'Well, there's nobody I'd like more for a sister-in-law.'

'How did you guess?' asked Ann, stopping on her way to the door.

'Peter's not the only one who can be the Great Detective,' retorted Margaret, smiling. 'He doesn't as a rule use lipstick and I see that he's got quite a fair amount of it on his mouth at the moment. You know my methods, Watson?'

Peter took his handkerchief from his pocket and vigorously rubbed his lips.

'You're quite right,' he said. 'I asked Ann to marry me and she said 'yes.''

'I'm very glad,' said his sister. 'I can't say I'm surprised. I've been wondering have long it would be before you asked her, and I dare say she has too. The symptoms were very obvious. You come and sit down, Ann. I'll make the tea.'

She went out to the kitchen and Peter looked at Ann.

'Were you?' he asked.

'Was I what?' she inquired.

'Wondering?'

'Well . . . ' She looked at him mischievously. 'I thought there was a good chance that you might, sooner or later.'

'I wish I'd known that,' he declared fervently. 'It would have been sooner.'

'I thought perhaps you might wait until after you'd solved the mystery,' she said.

'Oh, but I have,' he replied, to her surprise.

'You have?' she asked excitedly.

'I think I know who killed Mrs. Mallaby,' he said with calculated unconcern.

'But Peter — I don't understand . . . How do you know . . . When did you know . . . ?'

'It came to me quite suddenly,' said Peter airily. 'It's really very simple . . . '

'Peter, don't be smug and maddening,' said Ann. 'Tell me at once — who was it?'

Peter shook his head.

'I can't do that,' he declared. 'I've no proof — yet . . . '

'Are you going to be like the great

detective in fiction?' demanded Ann wrathfully. 'It's not fair, Peter . . . '

'I'll tell you directly I know for certain, darling,' said Peter. 'I promise . . . '

'When will that be?'

He thought for a moment.

'I should be certain by tomorrow night,' he said.

She came over to him and caught the lapels of his jacket.

'How long have you had this idea?' she said. 'When did it come to you?'

Peter looked a little confused.

'Well,' he said without looking at her. 'The idea struck me . . . just after you . . . just after we . . . h'm . . . '

'Peter!' she cried accusingly. 'Not *then*?' And when he nodded: 'Well, when a man *does* kiss me I *do* like to think that his mind's on the job . . . '

'Do you?' exclaimed Peter. 'Well, anything to oblige.'

And he offered a demonstration that left her in no doubt at all as to where his mind was at that particular moment.

★ ★ ★

Both Ann and Margaret tried their best to get Peter to tell them who he thought was responsible for the death of Mrs. Mallaby, but he stubbornly refused until, he said, he had put his idea to the test on the following day. No amount of persuasion or cajolery could budge him an inch.

It would not, he explained, be fair to say whom he suspected in case he should be wrong after all. He didn't think he was, but he might be. The sudden illuminating idea that had flashed to his mind was so simple, and yet accounted for everything, that he must be right.

'He's only being true to tradition,' said Margaret, when she found that all argument failed to move him. 'All the detectives in books develop this irritating habit. It's the hall-mark of the species. In the majority of cases it simply means that they don't know anything, but hope that should anything turn up it'll enhance their reputations if they pretend that they knew all the time.'

'You're not doing that, are you, Peter?' asked Ann suspiciously.

'No,' answered Peter. 'I assure you that I believe I know. I suddenly saw that we'd all made a glaring mistake. Once you see it, it's so easy you could kick yourself for not spotting it before.'

'I could kick you with the greatest pleasure,' said Margaret. 'I think you're being horribly mean. Both Ann and I are simply dying with curiosity, and you sit there like a — like a . . . '

'A deceased oyster?' suggested Ann.

'Or an Egyptian mummy,' said Margaret. 'Blown up with your own importance.'

But Peter steadfastly refused to say any more and was, in consequence, extremely unpopular for the rest of the evening.

Immediately after breakfast on the following morning he went out, leaving Ann and Margaret to overcome their curiosity as best they could. He did not return for lunch and they saw no more of him until tea time, when he came back looking tired and exhausted.

'Well?' demanded Ann and Margaret almost in the same breath, as he flung himself down on the settee and lighted a cigarette.

'Very well,' said Peter. 'I'm a little tired, that's all.'

'You know what we mean,' said his sister. 'Are you going to tell us what you've been up to?'

Peter shook his head.

'Not yet,' he answered. 'But I believe I'm right . . . '

'Look here, Peter,' said Ann. 'Do you want me to marry you?'

'Of course,' said Peter. 'More than anything in the world . . . '

'Then you'd better tell us all about it,' said Ann firmly. 'Otherwise . . . '

'That is blackmail,' remarked Peter.

'I don't care what it is, I want to know,' she retorted.

'Well, be patient a little longer and you shall hear all about it,' he said. 'I've got to go and see somebody and then . . . '

'Are you going out again?' demanded Margaret.

'Yes,' answered Peter. 'I have an appointment but I shan't be long.'

They looked at him curiously.

'I suppose,' said Ann, 'there's a good reason why you are behaving like this. Tell us one thing, will you?'

'That depends what it is,' said Peter cautiously.

'Is your idea connected with the five hundred pounds?' she asked.

He nodded.

'Very much so,' he answered. 'It's got everything to do with it. I always said that if we could find out what had happened to that, we should know all the rest.'

'And have you found out?' asked Margaret.

'Yes, I think I have,' said Peter complacently.

'You're the most exasperating man I've ever known,' exclaimed his sister. 'If I was Ann I'd think twice before I ever married you.'

★ ★ ★

Peter paused at the gate of the small house before he opened it and walked up the short path to the front door.

It was a fine night. The moon, a yellow rind, hung in a cold sky that was cloudless. There was a touch of frost in the air and Peter could see his breath smoking as he walked slowly up the path. The information he was seeking would clinch his theory one way or the other and he couldn't help a tinge of excitement as he raised his hand to the knocker.

Mr. Withers came to the door himself in answer to the knock. His small, monkey-like face was wrinkled into its usual harassed expression, but he forced a smile as he ushered Peter into the hall.

'Good evening, Hunt,' he said with his habitual slight stammer. 'What brings you here, eh? You're quite a stranger.'

'I want to ask you a question,' said Peter.

Mr. Withers looked at him doubtfully.

'We'd b-better go into the dining-room,' he said. 'My wife and daughter are in the s-sitting-room . . . '

'The dining-room will do admirably,' answered Peter. 'I shan't keep you very long.'

'Let me t-take your hat and coat,' said Mr. Withers hospitably.

Peter shed his coat and the little man

took it and his hat, and deposited them on an oak chest in the hall. Then he led the way into the dining-room.

'You'd l-like a drink, I expect,' said Mr. Withers, when he had seated Peter in an easy chair and shut the door. 'What will you have? Whisky, gin . . . '

Peter chose whisky, and the bank manager poured out two generous portions of Johnnie Walker.

'Water or soda?' he asked.

'Water, please,' said Peter. 'Soda spoils a good whisky.'

Mr. Withers added a small portion of water to each glass and brought one over to Peter.

'Thanks,' he said.

'I'm sorry I wasn't able to s-see you this afternoon when you called at the bank,' said Mr. Withers apologetically. 'I was so very busy. What was it you wished to ask me? N-nothing wrong with your a-account, I hope?'

'No,' answered Peter. 'Not as far as I'm aware. Why I wanted to see you has nothing to do with my account.'

Mr. Withers passed a nervous hand

over his wrinkled forehead and looked more perplexed than was habitual with him. But he said nothing, waiting for Peter to explain the reason for his visit.

'What I wanted to see you about,' said Peter, 'is this matter of five hundred pounds which Mrs. Mallaby drew from the bank on the Monday before she was killed . . .'

Mr. Withers's expression changed to one of surprise.

'I am afraid . . . I really don't think that I can discuss that,' he said hesitantly. 'You see . . . the business of the bank . . .'

'Was this the business of the bank?' asked Peter.

'Why, yes . . . of course.' Mr. Withers's astonishment grew. 'Mr. Buncombe has all the d-details relating to Mrs. M-Mallaby's account . . .'

'Not quite all the details,' said Peter quietly. 'Not all the details concerning that five hundred pounds at any rate.'

Mr. Withers put his glass down on the mantelpiece untasted.

'I d-don't know w-what you mean,' he stammered.

'I think you do,' said Peter. 'Look here, Withers, I'm damned sorry for you. I've come here tonight in a more or less friendly spirit to have it out with you.'

'To — to have it out with m-me?' repeated Mr. Withers, moistening his lips.

Peter nodded.

'Yes,' he replied. 'Without beating about the bush, there never was any five hundred pounds, was there? I mean Mrs. Mallaby never drew that money out of the bank at all, did she? The story you told Hockley and the cheque you gave him were both false. You forged that cheque yourself to cover up the fact that you'd taken five hundred pounds out of Mrs. Mallaby's account for your own uses. That's right, isn't it?'

The brown, monkey-like eyes stared at him. There was a sad and rather hopeless expression in them, but he said nothing.

'And you killed Mrs. Mallaby too, didn't you?' said Peter after a pause. 'You killed her because she had asked for a complete statement of her account, and you knew she'd find out what you had done?'

236

No word, no sound, only the hopeless, despairing fixed stare of those small brown eyes.

Peter swallowed his whisky at a gulp.

'I can guess why you did this,' he said gently, 'and I'm damned sorry — damned sorry . . .'

The small wrinkled face of Mr. Withers twitched all over. His eyelids blinked rapidly, and suddenly and unexpectedly he sank into the chair behind him and began to cry, softly at first and then more and more violently until the whole of his thin body was shaking with his sobs.

Peter looked on with compassionate embarrassment. All the nervous anxiety and worry of years, the strain and pent-up emotions, lack of sleep and overwork, had culminated in this sudden and complete breakdown. There was nothing he could do to alleviate the man's distress except to wait in silence until he grew calmer. He felt an intense pity for him. What he had done had not been for himself, but to satisfy the rapacious demands and greed of his family.

It was sad that this should be the end

of all those years of unselfish toil; half a lifetime of misplaced devotion.

It was not so much Withers who was to blame for the murder of Mrs. Mallaby as the wife and daughter whose thoughtless extravagance had prompted it.

Slowly the outburst dwindled and died, the racking sobs grew less frequent, and presently Mr. Withers raised his head.

He looked beaten and utterly exhausted.

Peter got up quietly, took the glass of whisky from the mantelpiece, and held it out to him.

'Drink this,' he said kindly. 'It'll pull you together.'

Mr. Withers grasped it with a shaking hand and swallowed its contents.

'I — I'm sorry,' he gasped unevenly. 'I — I'm very sorry. I m-must a-apologise . . . '

'Don't bother about that,' said Peter. 'I ought to apologise for having to be the cause . . . '

'How . . . how did you find . . . out?' whispered the bank manager almost inaudibly.

'It suddenly occurred to me,' explained

Peter, 'that the whole business of the five hundred pounds rested entirely on your unsubstantiated word and the evidence of the cheque. If the story of the five hundred pounds was false, and you had bolstered it up with a forged cheque, which you could quite easily have done with the aid of a signature from a genuine one, the natural inference was that you had appropriated the five hundred pounds for your own use, with the further inference that you had also killed Mrs. Mallaby. Unless she had died, the whole thing was bound to come out, and it was inconceivable to suppose that her death was a coincidence. It happened far too conveniently for that. I made one or two inquiries and found that you had recently settled a number of outstandings debts the amount of which came to very nearly five hundred pounds. Then I was sure . . .'

'Have you . . . i-informed the p-police?' asked Mr. Withers.

Peter shook his head.

'No, not yet,' he said. 'I thought I would tell you first.'

'Thank you,' murmured the little man mechanically.

'You realise that I shall have to tell Hockley,' said Peter. 'Much as I hate the idea. This is far too serious a thing to hush up.'

Mr. Withers bowed his head.

'I realise that,' he said.

'I shall take no further steps in the matter until tomorrow morning,' said Peter.

He looked at the other steadily and Mr. Withers nodded.

'Thank you,' he said again. 'You are quite right, you know. I — I didn't think anybody w-would find out. I was at m-my wits' end for m-money . . . I'd got myself into r-rather a m-mess . . . Some of m-my creditors were threatening l-legal proceedings. I took the m-money but I'd really no intention of k-killing her. I hope you w-will believe that. B-But she got s-suspicious, I d-don't know how, and d-demanded a full statement of her account. I would not have b-been able to cover up my defalcation . . . '

'If you'd come to me,' said Peter, 'I

would have helped you.'

'It never occurred to me,' said Mr. Withers. 'So few people are interested in other people's worries.' He sighed. 'It is n-not a kind world, you know.'

There was something infinitely pathetic in the tone of his voice.

No, thought Peter, it has not been a kind world for you. And yet you have done your duty — more than your duty — even though it led to murder . . .

'I was thinking of my f-family,' went on the little man. 'The disgrace w-would have b-been dreadful for them . . . '

Not himself. Always that family who had sucked every atom of life and energy from him until there was little left and still wanted more . . .

'I knew of her habit of g-going to the church every afternoon,' continued the bank manager, 'and I w-waited for her. Nobody saw m-me go or c-come back . . . '

'How did you know exactly the spot to inflict a fatal wound?' asked Peter curiously.

'I used to be in the St. John's

Ambulance Brigade,' replied Mr. Withers. 'I m-made a study of first-aid and anatomy then.'

'It was a penknife, wasn't it?' asked Peter, and the other nodded.

'Yes, it was a p-penknife,' he repeated dully.

There was a step outside the door and Diana came in quickly.

'Mother wants to know how long dinner will be,' she began, and then she saw Peter. 'Oh, good evening, Mr. Hunt.'

Peter bowed.

'I'm afraid you'll have to g-get dinner for yourselves tonight m'dear,' said Mr. Withers, forcing a faint smile. 'I shall b-be too busy . . . '

Diana's face clouded.

'Can't you do whatever you've got to do after?' she demanded.

Her father shook his head.

'I'm afraid I c-can't,' he said.

'Well, you might have let us know earlier,' said Diana crossly. 'I'm starving and it's going to make it very late . . . '

Mr. Withers sighed wearily. Even at this

crisis in his life the habit of years asserted itself.

'I'll try and see what I can do,' he said.

Peter felt his temper rise. He would have dearly liked to tell both Diana and her mother what he thought of them. A few home truths would do them good. Neither of them, in spite of everything, were fit to tie that pathetic little man's bootlaces.

'I must be going,' he said shortly, stifling his desire to let his temper have its fling.

'I'll come to the door with you,' said Mr. Withers, getting up.

'Good night, Mr. Hunt,' said Diana.

Peter, rudely as he admitted to himself, ignored her. He followed the thin figure of the bank manager to the hall and collected his hat and coat. It had been a nasty job. He began to wish fervently that he had never started to find the murderer of Mrs. Mallaby.

'Remember,' he said in a low voice, 'I shall do nothing until tomorrow morning. I hope you — understand?'

'I d-do, and I'm very grateful,' said Mr.

Withers earnestly.

'Well, goodbye,' said Peter awkwardly, and held out his hand. The little man took it with a quick nervous pressure.

'Goodbye,' he said.

He waited until Peter had disappeared down the road and then he closed the door and made his way slowly to the kitchen.

He cooked the dinner after all that night and his wife and daughter ate it with enjoyment. They had no knowledge of what emotions were going on behind the usual worried face of the little man who had slaved for years that they might live in comfort.

But there was no early tea on the following morning to stimulate them to wakefulness. They waited for some time in surprised annoyance at this unusual lack of attention on the part of Mr. Withers, and then in an excess of irritation, and a dressing-gown, Diana went to discover the cause of this unwonted tardiness on the part of her father . . .

The small narrow bed in his small

cheerless room, the smallest in the house, was empty. Diana went downstairs but the fire had not been lighted nor the grate cleared up.

Unable to understand this, Diana searched the house but there was no sign of her father anywhere. A little alarmed, she hurried up the stairs and reported the matter to her mother.

'Not in the house?' said Mrs. Withers. 'But that's ridiculous. He must be there somewhere. Have you looked in the garden? Perhaps he's chopping wood.'

But there was no sign of Mr. Withers in the garden either.

'It's really most inconsiderate of him,' said Mrs. Withers irritably. 'If he had to go out early the least he could have done was to bring us our tea. You'd better go and make it, Diana.'

Rather sullenly, for she was not used to doing anything, Diana obeyed.

When they had had their tea — it was not so well-made as they were used to — Mrs. Withers decided to get up.

'Go and run me a bath, Diana,' she said. 'I cannot understand what can have happened to your father. I don't remember his ever behaving like this before.'

Diana went, reluctantly, but she was back in less than a minute, white-faced and anxious.

'I can't get into the bathroom,' she announced. 'The door's locked on the inside and I've banged on it but there's no sound . . . '

'You're sure it hasn't just stuck?' asked her mother.

Diana shook her head.

'Didn't you look in the bathroom before?' asked Mrs. Withers. 'When you were looking for your father?'

Again Diana shook her head.

The usual placid expression, that was rather like a sleek cat, fled from Mrs. Withers's face. She got out of bed and pulled on her dressing-gown.

'Surely your father can't have been taken ill,' she muttered. 'I can't understand why you didn't try the bathroom before . . . '

She hurried out of the bedroom with Diana at her heels and down the passage to the bathroom door. It was a half-glass door, the upper panel being of opaque glass so that it was impossible to see in from the outside or outside from within.

Mrs. Withers banged on the door loudly.

'Are you in there, Horace?' she demanded, but there was no reply.

The worried expression on Mrs. Withers's face deepened.

'What had we better do?' asked Diana rather helplessly.

'We'll have to break open the door,' said her mother. 'The easiest way will be to smash the glass.'

'I'll go and get a hammer,' said Diana, and she hurried away.

Mrs. Withers waited anxiously, her mind in a confused whirl. Perhaps her husband had had a heart attack or a stroke? What would happen to her and Diana if he should die? There would be no money, only the insurance, and that wasn't for much. What would become of them? She still had no thought for the man who had devoted the greater part of his life to her comfort, giving her all he could and more. Her thoughts, her worries, were all for herself . . .

Diana came back with a hammer.

'Break it near the lock,' said her mother. 'Then we can put a hand in and turn the key.'

Diana struck at the glass and with a tinkling crash it splintered. She put her hand in the jagged hole, felt for the key and turned it. Pushing the door open, they both crowded into the little room.

At her first glimpse, Mrs. Withers screamed and clutched her daughter by the arm.

Mr. Withers lay in the bath and all the outcries and beseechings would never wake him again. The water was red with the life blood which had flowed from the severed arteries in his wrists. They scarcely recognised him, for all the worry and anxiety had been smoothed away and there was an expression of peace on his face such as they had never seen there before . . .

11

Superintendent Hockley was pardonably annoyed when he heard the news.

'You knew that he would do something of this sort, sir,' he said accusingly when Peter had related the full story, 'when you saw him last night.'

'I hoped that he would,' admitted Peter candidly. 'I gave him the chance when I said I wasn't going to do anything until this morning. I hoped that he'd understand. Apparently he did.'

'You should have come to me first,' said the superintendent severely.

'So that you could have arrested him and dragged him through all the misery and disgrace of a trial?' said Peter. 'He'd suffered enough during his life, poor little devil. And what difference does it make? He's given his life for the life he took and that's all the law could have demanded.'

'It was wrong all the same, sir,' said

Hockley, shaking his head. 'I suppose it can't be helped though, now.'

'Look here,' said Peter. 'Withers was a poor, down-trodden little drudge, without a soul to call his own. What he did, he did for the sake of that selfish and greedy family of his. They sucked him dry of every penny he could earn and demanded more . . . '

'That's as may be, sir,' interrupted Hockley stolidly. 'But he should have had the strength of character to tell them to keep within bounds. Other men have to. He just needed a little firmness of will . . . '

'Firmness of will?' echoed Peter. 'He hadn't any will left to exert any firmness with. You saw him. The husk of a man, worn out with overwork and constant anxiety.'

'That doesn't justify murder,' said the superintendent stubbornly.

'I know it doesn't,' retorted Peter, 'but it explains it. I'm not trying to justify him. Don't think that. There's nothing anyone could say or do that would justify him in what he did. But I do say that he deserved the chance to find his own way out, which I gave him.'

Hockley shrugged his shoulders.

'I can't say that I see eye to eye with you over that, sir,' he declared, 'but it's not much use arguing over it now. The thing's done, and there it is. But I do think, when you hit on this idea of yours about the money and Withers, that you should have come and told me. The law's the law, and if everybody started taking it into their own hands, it 'ud lead to a pretty kettle of fish an' no mistake.'

'Well, let's forget it,' said Peter soothingly, realising that he would never get Hockley to see his point of view if they argued until doomsday. 'You haven't got much to grumble about, you know. You've succeeded in solving the mystery and finding the murderer, and it ought to be a feather in your cap with the powers that be. It was more a lucky shot of mine than anything else, finding out the truth, and you can keep me out of it altogether.'

Perhaps the knowledge that he would get the credit did more than a little to appease the disgruntled superintendent.

At any rate his manner was distinctly more mollified when he spoke again.

'Whether is was a lucky shot or not, sir,' he said, 'it was smart, and I don't mind saying so. It never occurred to me that Withers might have made up all that story about the cheque an' Mrs. Mallaby wanting the money all in one-pound notes. I took it for granted that he was telling the truth. Because he was a bank manager with the background of the bank, I suppose, if you understand what I mean?'

Peter nodded.

'I understand perfectly,' he said. 'It was the sort of thing you wouldn't question coming from that source. Once you *did* question it, everything dropped neatly into place.'

'He might easily have got away with it,' said Hockley. 'He was lucky on the afternoon of the murder. Somebody might have seen him coming from or going to, the church. He took a risk there.'

'He just took a chance,' said Peter. 'He wouldn't have been capable of thinking out a really clever murder. He hadn't the brain. Look at the way he died. It wasn't very original to cut the arteries in his wrists and just lie in that bath and wait . . . '

★ ★ ★

'I'm glad you gave the poor little man a chance,' said Margaret, when she and Ann had been told the full story. 'I'm sure he deserved that. Well, Mrs. Withers and Diana will have to go and work for their living now, I suppose. There won't be any money, will there?'

'I shouldn't think there would be much,' said Peter. 'I should imagine that Withers was insured, but, of course, I've no idea for how much.'

'I hope they both have to work very hard and get very little for it,' said Margaret vindictively. 'It'll serve them right. Goodness knows what they'll do though. I shouldn't think they would be much good at anything. Diana might get a job as a chorus girl or a model . . . '

'That's not so easy as it appears — not

these days,' remarked Ann. 'They want more than a good figure and a pretty face.'

'She'll have to look for a rich husband,' said Peter. 'In which case, if she's lucky enough to find one, Mrs. Withers will settle herself on them and take more than her share of anything that happens to be going. Meanwhile, I hope they both have a pretty rough time. They deserve it for the way they treated that poor little man.'

The suicide of Mr. Withers caused a sensation in Long Manton. The facts were all round the village with the rapidity of a forest fire and quite a number of very unkind remarks were made about the widow and her daughter.

People remembered how the harassed little man had worked to keep them in comparative luxury and their sympathies were nearly all for him.

Miss Ginch and Miss Dewsnap were among the few who openly expressed horror at what he had done.

'A bank manager too,' said Miss Dewsnap, shaking her thin head, 'Thank heavens *I* never had any money in his bank or I might have been the victim.'

'Yes indeed,' said Miss Ginch, clasping her hands and raising her eyes to the ceiling — the conversation took place in the post-office, 'I have never been fortunate enough to have enough money to put in any bank . . . '

'You had hopes at one time, though, didn't you dear?' said Miss Dewsnap with a world of meaning in her look if not in her voice.

'I don't know what you mean by *that*,' said Miss Ginch sharply.

'I'm sure you thought your *dear* friend, Mrs. Mallaby would remember you,' said Miss Dewsnap kindly. 'It must have been a very great disappointment.'

There was so much truth in this statement that Miss Ginch reddened.

'I would never have accepted anything from that woman,' she declared. 'Never. No one could possibly have been so cruelly deceived about anybody as I was about her.'

'Well, she never gave you the chance to refuse, did she?' asked Miss Dewsnap sweetly, and for several days afterwards there was a distinct coolness between them.

It was on the day following the discovery of Mr. Withers's death that Superintendent Hockley exploded his bombshell.

Peter was working in his study, feeling rather lost and unsettled now that Ann had gone back to London, when Hockley was announced.

He greeted the superintendent genially, but with a faint underlying surprise, for he wondered what could have brought him.

'You look rather astonished to see me, Mr. Hunt,' said Hockley shrewdly. 'You'll be more astonished when you learn why I'm here.'

'What's the news?' asked Peter. 'Don't tell me there's been another murder?'

'No, thank goodness,' said Hockley. 'We've got the first one to clear up yet . . .'

'You mean — Mrs. Mallaby?' exclaimed Peter, and when Hockley nodded: 'But that's cleared up. Withers . . .'

'It wasn't Withers,' interrupted the

superintendent. 'I'm sorry, sir, but your idea was all wrong . . . '

'All wrong?' echoed Peter incredulously. 'How can it be all wrong? Withers admitted it. He killed himself because . . . '

'It's all wrong, sir,' repeated Hockley. 'I can't help what he admitted or anything. He could *not* have killed Mrs. Mallaby.'

Peter stared at him. This was nonsense. This was impossible.

'But he did,' he said feebly.

Hockley shook his head emphatically.

'No, sir, he did not,' he repeated. 'He couldn't have done it. At the time the murder must have been committed, he was talking to Mr. Totts, the chief chashier.'

'Are you *sure* of this?' asked Peter, thoroughly bewildered.

Hockley nodded.

'There must be a mistake,' said Peter. 'There *must* be. Totts has muddled up the time.'

'He swears that on that Friday afternoon, Withers was talking to him from a quarter to four to a quarter to five. They were trying to find a slight

257

discrepancy in the cash — only a matter of a few shillings . . . '

'It's just not possible,' broke in Peter. 'Withers confessed. He committed suicide. Why should he do that if he was innocent . . . '

'Maybe he wanted to shield someone,' said the superintendent.

Peter frowned.

'The only people he would have sacrificed himself to shield,' he said, 'would be either his wife or his daughter. They could neither of them have done the murder . . . '

Hockley gave him a quick sidelong look.

'What makes you so sure of that, sir?' he asked.

'They couldn't,' declared Peter. 'They had no opportunity to forge that cheque . . . '

'I don't altogether agree with you,' interrupted the superintendent, shaking his head. 'I suppose they both had the run of the bank? They could pop in and out when they liked to see Withers. Suppose one of 'em pinched a cheque form and forged Mrs. Mallaby's signature . . . '

'Rubbish,' broke in Peter rudely. 'I'm sorry, Hockley, but it is rubbish, you know. They might have forged the signature, but how could they have cashed the cheque without Withers knowing? They couldn't . . . '

Hockley was forced to agree that it would have been next to impossible.

'Totts is trying to whitewash Withers,' went on Peter. 'That's the only explanation. He's lying to save his friend's reputation.'

'Well, he sticks to it, sir,' replied Hockley with a grimace. 'I thought that and tried to shake his story but he wouldn't budge. From a quarter to four to a quarter to five he and Withers were at the bank together. That's his story and he's sticking to it.'

And Mr. Totts continued to stick to it. All the questioning couldn't make him budge. When Mr. Totts's assertion leaked out the village ranged itself into two camps. There were those who believed him and those who did not and many were the heated arguments in the Fox and Hounds respecting the matter.

It was discovered, too, that poor Withers had failed to pay the last premium on his life policy — it had been two months overdue at the time of his death — and so there was no money from that source for the widow and daughter.

Faced with nothing except the contents of the house they lived in — the house itself was only rented — Mrs. Withers and Diana sold the furniture and, with the meagre capital thus realised, took a cheap bed-sitting-room in Bloomsbury, and the village of Long Manton knew them no more.

But it was not quite the last it heard of them.

In the first week of December of that year, one of the London dailies carried a paragraph concerning two women — mother and daughter — who had been arrested by a store detective in one of the big stores for shop-lifting.

The name of the accused persons was — Withers.

'Serve them right,' said Margaret, when Peter showed her the paragraph. 'I'm very glad.'

And she wasn't the only one who felt the same way.

Mr. Buncombe tried hard to get Ann to accept the large estate left by her mother, but she would listen to none of his arguments until, hearing that she was engaged to Peter Hunt, he hit on the bright idea of suggesting that it should be held in trust for her children. This, after a consultation with Peter, she agreed to.

Mr. and Mrs. Conway, after several months of uneasy speculation as to whether her connection with the Lucas case was going to leak out, and finding as time went by that there was no sign of this disaster happening, began to breathe more freely and, eventually, found something of the peace that they had enjoyed before.

Mrs. Bramber continued to suffer spasmodically from her unidentifiable complaint, consume large quantities of Turkish delight, and talk nostalgically about the joys and beauties of her beloved India. The Reverend Mr. Popkiss gradually recovered from the shock of his daughter's mental derangement, although there seemed little likelihood that she could ever be cured. Mr. Penny presided over the bar at the Fox and Hounds with all his habitual geniality, and Long Manton after its period of notoriety, gradually settled back once more into its previous oblivion, although it was not quite the same as it had been. There was a little more tolerance among the people who composed its small population, one to another, and if only for this reason, Mrs. Mallaby had not died in vain. In some queer way the forces of evil, which had hung so heavily over the place, had exhausted themselves and become dissipated . . .

Peter and Ann were married on New Year's Day and went abroad for their honeymoon, leaving Margaret to superintend the redecoration of the house in their absence. She herself was going to move into a cottage on the outskirts of the village — a pretty, creeper-covered place that rejoiced in the name of 'Hollybush,' presumably because there was no sign of that evergreen tree within several miles.

Manton Lodge was sold with all its contents and was later converted into a school, so that where once the shadow of death had passed, grim and terrible, removing in its passing the selfish woman who had lived her lonely existence there, there was now the happy sound of laughing children to lift the last gloomy memories and disperse the last shadow.

THE END

We do hope that you have enjoyed reading this large print book.

Did you know that all of our titles are available for purchase?

We publish a wide range of high quality large print books including:
Romances, Mysteries, Classics
General Fiction
Non Fiction and Westerns

Special interest titles available in large print are:
The Little Oxford Dictionary
Music Book, Song Book
Hymn Book, Service Book

Also available from us courtesy of Oxford University Press:
Young Readers' Dictionary
(large print edition)
Young Readers' Thesaurus
(large print edition)

For further information or a free brochure, please contact us at:
Ulverscroft Large Print Books Ltd.,
The Green, Bradgate Road, Anstey,
Leicester, LE7 7FU, England.
Tel: (00 44) 0116 236 4325
Fax: (00 44) 0116 234 0205

Other titles in the
Linford Mystery Library:

THE DARK BOATMAN

John Glasby

Five chilling tales: a family's history is traced back for four centuries — with no instance of a death recorded . . . The tale of an aunt who wanders out to the graveyard each night . . . A manor house is built on cursed land, perpetuating the evil started there long ago . . . The fate of a doctor, investigating the ravings of a man sent mad by the things he has witnessed . . . The evil residing at Dark Point lighthouse where the Devil himself was called up . . .

CASE OF THE DIXIE GHOSTS

A. A. Glynn

America's bloody Civil War is over, leaving a legacy of bitterness, intrigues and villainy — not all acted out on the American continent. A ship from the past docks in Liverpool, England; the mysterious Mr. Fortune, carrying a burden of secrets, slips ashore and disappears into the fogs of winter. And in London, detective Septimus Dacers finds that helping an American girl in distress plunges him into combat with the Dixie Ghosts, and brings him face-to-face with threatened murder — his own.